THE INVENTION OF DR CAKE

The Invention
of Dr Cake

ANDREW MOTION

faber and faber

First published in 2003
by Faber and Faber Limited
3 Queen Square London WC1N 3AU

Typeset by Faber and Faber Limited
Printed in England by Mackays of Chatham plc,
Chatham, Kent

A CIP record for this book
is available from the British Library

ISBN 0–571–21631–5

2 4 6 8 10 9 7 5 3 1

For Alan Hollinghurst

As in that trance of wondrous thought I lay,
This was the tenor of my waking dream: –
    Shelley, 'The Triumph of Life'

Contents

FOREWORD

Wordsworth says somewhere that he thought of himself as a man with certain powers of imagination, but limited powers of invention. In other words: he knew what to do with a story once he'd got hold of one, but was no good at making things up from scratch.

I often think of this when I'm wondering why I like writing biography. I tell myself it's because the story is *there*: something to be worked for, of course, and which might require long hours in libraries, in conversation, even travelling the world. But essentially and properly it's a pre-existing thing – a road-map, a ground-plan, a grid – which serves as a basis for my ideas and interpretations. To put it another way: I like writing biography because it's a balancing act – a mixture of the known and the unknowable, of truth and speculation.

But like all balancing acts, it can't be sustained for ever. Each of us has a worm in our brain which demands strangeness and change, not endless repetition, and I'm no exception. After more than fifteen years of writing orthodox Lives – beginning at the beginning, going on to the end, then stopping – I've got impatient with the process, and to a limited extent with the results as well. Aren't human beings always odder than their histories suggest? Aren't the connections between experience and achievement always more oblique? And don't the traditional methods of biography (those hours sleuthing in archives) lead us back again and again to the same subjects, while leaving others out in the cold, or languishing in footnotes?

Recently I've cast around for new ways of doing things. Six or seven years ago, when I was writing my Life of John Keats, I glimpsed in the background the sinister figure of Thomas Griffiths Wainewright, a painter and a murderer who was notorious in his day, but has since faded from view. I decided to write about him next – for his own peculiar sake, and because there wasn't much surviving information about him, which in turn meant I had an unusual amount of space in which to manoeuvre. I felt that Wainewright would encourage me to make a different kind of connection between invention and imagination.

I published the results four years ago. But I knew at once that I had more to do, partly because not even Wainewright had allowed me to ask all the questions I had in my mind about secrecy, and partly because I'd discovered someone else during my researches, whom I felt would stretch still further the way I thought about the connection between life and art. His name was William Tabor.

Tabor didn't know Wainewright well – they had dinner together a few times in the late 1820s, that's all. But since hard facts about Wainewright are so rare, I'd felt bound to investigate this contact, and was led in due course to the library of the Royal College of Surgeons, where Tabor's papers were deposited soon after his death in 1850. When I began to look at them properly, I saw that the real fascination of Tabor's story didn't lie with the man himself, but with someone he had met: a certain Dr John Cake.

But first things first. Who was William Tabor? Devotees of the Romantics might have heard of him as a doctor who campaigned for medical reform. Anthology-readers will know a handful of his poems. Biography buffs will know that he was on goodish terms with Charles Lamb, and shook hands with Coleridge one winter afternoon in Highgate in 1832. But apart from that he's been forgotten. He was obviously a clever man, but equally obviously he was discreet as a clam. Maybe that's what made him a good doctor – and a good friend.

This means Tabor's life story looks simple but feels slippery. His father was an architect (a Scot, also called William) who was born on a farm in the Lowlands with the inspiring name of Phantasie, and migrated south as he searched for work during the 1790s. He ended up in Finchley, then a village beyond the northern rim of London, building houses for well-to-do men who were beginning to see the point of working in the city and rearing their families in the country.

Very little is known about William junior's childhood, beyond the facts that he was born on 26 July 1802, went to the local school in Finchley, was apprenticed to the local apothecary, and trained to be a doctor in Edinburgh. We don't know where he lived during this time – probably with relatives of his father – and we don't know what he was like. All we can do is assume he was diligent, practical and law-abiding, and realise these are the very things which have driven him from the public record.

Tabor qualified as a doctor in 1830 and immediately bought a practice in Finchley (helped by a legacy from his father, who had died ten years earlier). He moved in with his mother and worked from his childhood home. Here at last the shape of his life gets clearer, since a part of the house is still standing. There's a grey stone façade overlooking the main street – endlessly shaken by traffic – with a pretty pattern of red bricks around the windows and front door, and niches either side of the door, where statues might once have stood. This combination of weight and lightness is typical Tabor – but like a good deal else about him, it turns out to be deceptive. A bomb, which fell on the back lane in 1940, blew down everything except this front wall and also destroyed the outbuildings, where Tabor kept his apothecary's 'counter'.

Tabor himself may be hard to pin down, but it's all too easy to imagine what he put up with in his work: an endless stream of tubercular patients coughing their lungs out; labourers carted in from the fields with their limbs sliced or crushed or skewered; sick children howling in their mothers' arms. Even the slighter cases must have been hideously depressing: the daily round of upset stomachs and runny noses, of nervousness and hypochondria, or doling out pills everyone knew were useless. Tabor lived through a revolution in medicine, but most of his methods were still extremely primitive. More

4

often than not, he was offering councils of despair, like every other doctor of the time.

If he felt frustrated by this, he never said so: he just recycled disappointment into hard work – and pride. Throughout his life in Finchley, he kept a log of his visits to and from patients, and these volumes (nearly two dozen in all) form the bulk of his Archive in the Royal College. They are an amazingly complete record of the life of a doctor in the Romantic period. They show how Tabor wanted to see the health of the whole country improved, not just the lives of his friends and neighbours, and how he set about making it happen with a terrific blast of Victorian energy. The culmination of his efforts is his *Survey of the Conditions and Health of the Rural Poor* (1846). This gigantic compendium was much admired when it was first published, and became for a while a popular handbook of ills and remedies. These days it's nothing more than a curiosity, but for all that, it still tells us something about Tabor: how fastidious he was, and how controlled.

Even someone so nearly saintly must please themselves, which Tabor did in his own determined way. While other twenty-somethings were off courting, or enjoying the countryside that still flourished around Finchley in those days, he turned towards London and more sober sorts of entertainment. It's not clear whether he wrote poetry during this time; if he did, no manuscripts have survived. We do know, though, that by 1830 he was already friendly with Lamb. Most likely, Tabor had offered an article to the *London Magazine* and the editor thought he was interesting enough to meet, then made other introductions.

Tabor doesn't give much of himself away in his poems. In fact the first of his two collections, called simply *Poems* (1829), is positively austere – the tone is dry as biscuit, and there are no surviving drafts (which might show how his mind worked), only the single fair copy that F. H. Greene used for his Collected Edition of 1913. This means the writing feels oddly disembodied – yet in a sense its origins are perfectly obvious. *Poems* is written by someone with a sharp eye, a good ear, and a mind that has been over-whelmed by a more powerful talent. By Wordsworth. On almost every page, a Cumbrian tramp or a homeless sol-dier wanders through the lanes around Finchley and philosophises about his fate. They still use their Lake-language (very plain) and their early Romantic forms (mostly ballads), and the contrast between the way they think and their surroundings is often frankly ridiculous. However hard he tries, Tabor can't make Finchley Common feel like a windswept mountain.

But there are things to be said in favour of *Poems* as well. For one thing, it's more skilful than most second-rate Romantic writing: Tabor knows how to keep stories going, and where to end them. There's something touch-ing about its seriousness, too – which probably has some-thing to do with his life as a doctor. Even though he never looked at his own career directly in his poems, and never described his patients or the treatments he offered them, there's still an impressive gravity about his moralisings. At the end of 'The Pedlar', for instance:

6

> And thus it is I come to speak
> The Truth with this last breath:
> We spend our lives pursuing Life
> But only find our death.

Twenty-two years after *Poems* had appeared, and a month before he died, Tabor published his second and final collection: *Hyperion and Other Poems*. His critics, in so far as he has any, usually refer to this gap as a 'silence', but this is misleading. The *London Magazine* may have used him only twice, but when it folded he soon found a home in other, more specialist journals. In fact hardly a year went by without him publishing something – an article, an essay, a long letter to an editor – on some aspect of rural poverty and its effect on health. The 1832 Reform Act, and the campaign for the repeal of the Corn Laws, goaded him into especially frantic activity. He published six long pieces in 1833 alone – a total of 150,000 words, and every line stuffed with good intentions. More hospitals, new and hygienic ward-plans, reviews of familiar operations (such as amputation), a study of the spleen, even recommendations about the treatment of tubercular patients which anticipate the great discoveries Koch made fifty-odd years later.

The extent of Tabor's medical writings helps us to understand why he didn't have much in the way of a private life, let alone the time to produce more poems. In his first volume there is a stilted elegy to his father, 'W.G.T.', which says that he (William senior) 'did prove/ His life on our turning earth/ Was well-equipped for love'. The book's other 'personal' lyrics are just as buttoned-up:

they're not addressed to a particular living person, but to an artificial idea of 'Beauty'. This isn't to say Tabor never had close contact with women, just that nothing is known about this part of his life. He never married, and when he appears in the diaries and correspondence of his friends (including the journal of Lady Elizabeth Carmichael, his neighbour in Finchley), he's always the stern representative of his profession.

All this makes the final volume of poetry a puzzle. Whereas his early poems are severe almost to the point of seeming bloodless, the late ones are oppositely lush and Keatsian – as the title warns us they might be. Tabor's enemies (and he has more enemies than friends, if we count indifference as a form of hostility) call him a fake. A poor-man's Chatterton. A con-man, who switched his loyalty from a first to a second generation Romantic. They don't care that his 'Hyperion' starts from the moment at which Keats abandoned his own poem – the emergence of Apollo 'with a pang/ As hot as death's is chill'. Nor that the Hyperion story was tackled by several Romantic poets other than Keats: Barry Cornwall, for instance. No, as far as his critics are concerned, Tabor is just an off-shoot of the Cockney prodigy. His poems are parasites.

In fact there are at least two interesting things about the book. Apart from anything else, it shows how the Keatsian style – opulent, velvety, swooning – outlived Keats himself. Tennyson's first book, which appeared in 1830, only nine years after Keats's death, proves the point. It's just as luxurious, and was reviled in very similar terms, sometimes by the same people who had jeered at Keats. ('It is a better and a wiser thing to be a starved apothecary than a starved poet,' one critic had told Keats; 'so back to the shop Mr John, back to the "plasters, pills and ointment boxes"', etc.) But as Tennyson weathered this storm, and took off into heroic narratives like 'Tithonus' and 'Ulysses', he struck the true, popular note of early Victorian verse: more sonorous than Keats, and in that sense duller, but similar all the same.

Then there are the poems themselves. The best bits of Tabor's 'Hyperion' are pretty well known. The flakes of ice which settle in Saturn's hair 'like petals quenched in amber beams'. The rose 'oozing scent/ As if self-satisfied by what it knew'. The moment Apollo defeats the ancient gods and gives a 'heart-expanding roar/ That set the whole of heaven ringing loud/ And made its night-birds silent at the sound'. Details like these remind us of the advice Keats gave Shelley to 'load every rift with ore', and they appear on page after page. Not just in 'Hyperion', but in the 'Hymn to Pomona', the narrative of Penelope, and the translation-extract from the *Orlando Furioso*.

If this were all Tabor had to offer, it would probably be enough to earn him his small niche in history. But there's something else as well. Just as Keats is always balancing pleasure against pain in his poems (the deathless bird and the dying 'youth' in the 'Ode to a Nightingale'), so is Tabor. His poems are beautiful, but saturated with grief. The bizarre 'Ode to Lethe' is a good example. Although every stanza is crammed with lovely details – the reedy river bank, the mossy boulders, the kingfisher on its branch – Tabor obviously wanted the poem to be read as a meditation on suffering. Hence the four rhetorical questions which end it (and echo Keats's 'Ode on a Grecian Urn'):

> What Beauty now could lure me back to life?
> What face? What tender-lifted hand?
> What brighter dark than this approaching shore?

The questions Tabor wants answered here are the ones which underlie all Romantic poetry. What is the value of a self? Does pain shape our personalities for good, or for ill? Can love face down death? And – last but not least – can artists keep their faith in art, when they know how their own story will end? For Tabor himself, the answer was obviously 'No'. In the final poem of *Hyperion*, the twelve-line 'Farewell', he tells us his work will turn out to be worthless 'dust'. Most writers would be incapable of saying such a thing without striking a false note, either because they don't believe their own self-deprecation, or because they expect readers to reject it. But there's no such hollowness in this case – which makes the lyric one of Tabor's best, as well as confirming his integrity. The humane doctor is apparently the same creature as the principled poet.

Apparently. But there's still the question: how did Tabor manage his sudden late burst of sensuality? Where did it come from? To answer this, we have to go back to the man – to the biography which has never been written and which (given the huge and unfillable gaps in our knowledge of him) probably never will be written. In its place we have only a pencil drawing, unsigned, but dated 1843. This came to light in 1937, when G. M. Hawkins was preparing his article on the *Survey of the Health and Conditions of the Rural Poor* (which eventually appeared in the *British Medical Journal*, Vol. LVI, No.3), and is clearly intended to show a person of contradictions. Tabor is sitting in a complicated wooden chair beside an ivy-covered wall. He's wearing a charcoal flannel suit, the jacket creased under the arms, his waistcoat cushioning the bright chain of his fob-watch, the trousers bagging away from the left knee where it crosses the right. His boots are gleaming and supple, laced to the ankle; his bow-tie is a large spotted affair.

And the face? The face is slightly smudged, as though he'd just that moment lost patience with the artist, and asked him to hurry up. A heavy square skull; sandy hair oiled back with a central parting, and falling over the collar; large grave eyes; a thick-lipped, effeminate mouth; what might be a small mole, or possibly a defect in the paper, to the right of the nose; the nose itself aquiline, hawkish; the whole effect paradoxical: stern yet sensual, withdrawn but shining with appetite – almost with greed.

Tabor thought very little of his contemporaries' interest in phrenology. 'It is not the way we appear that makes us what we are,' he wrote in 1842, 'but the health of our interior selves. This in turn may affect the face we present to the world, in which is advertised our condition, but to assume that we are condemned to a certain personality by the set of our eyes, or the depth of our brows, is to deny ourselves a fundamental liberty.' In spite of this, Tabor's

11

face is highly suggestive – a delicate mixture of candour and concealment, of mingled guilt and pleasure, of affability as well as selfishness.

Which brings us, in an appropriately roundabout way, to Tabor's friendship with the elusive Dr Cake. They first met when Tabor was working on the *Survey of the Health and Conditions of the Rural Poor*, trying to beef up his case histories by soliciting the opinion of other doctors who shared his interests. He quotes at regular intervals from colleagues in Finchley, and sometimes further afield as well. From a Dr Liddell of Enfield, for instance, who thought he could cure typhoid by putting pig's liver on the chest of his patients. From a Dr Warner of Harringay, who thought that if you slipped a porridge of dock leaves inside bandages, it would help bones to mend more quickly. And from a Dr John Cake in north Essex, who held the enlightened belief that 'kindness to the suffering is as likely to bring a good reward in some cases as a whole cabinet of medicine'.

Generally speaking, it's the job of a Foreword to give information and resolve difficulties. But as I've already said, this is not an orthodox account of a life; it's one which balances invention and imagination. And that being the case, Dr Cake should be left to do most of his speaking for himself – or, at least, to appear as Tabor saw him. The bare facts of his life are easily told. He was born in 1795, like Tabor he trained as a doctor (but in London not in Edinburgh), and in the early 1830s he bought a practice in Woodham, on the border of Essex and Suffolk. He spent the rest of his life in this small village, published regularly in medical journals (which is how Tabor came across him), living quietly and alone with his housekeeper, Mrs Reilly. He died in 1844. What is not so easily told is the story behind these bare facts – a story which is at once extraordinary and elusive. In other words, everything we know about Dr Cake is revealed in the documents that follow. Everything mysterious about him is suggested by them as well.

ONE

John Cake died on 17 August 1844, and was buried a week later in the graveyard of St Mary's, Woodham, Essex. Shortly afterwards, William Tabor wrote an obituary for the local paper, the *Messenger*, which was published in Halstead, near Woodham, between 1832 and 1851. At around the same time, Tabor also wrote a less dutiful, more personal account of the funeral – apparently for no eyes but his own. These two items are pinned together in the Archive of the Royal College of Surgeons.

From the *Messenger*, 27 August 1844:

The loss of a man whose life has been of value to his community is always a matter for regret, and when that community is a small one, the loss will seem especially severe. Dr John Cake, whose funeral took place at St Mary's Church, Woodham, on Thursday last, following his death on 17 August, will be mourned by all those who knew him. As a doctor in times of suffering, as a wise counsellor in times of trouble, and as a friend in times of contentment, Dr Cake had few peers. The fact that he chose to live quietly, away from the bustle of cities, established no limit to his compassion. In everything he did, he showed himself a man of the widest sympathies.

John Cake was born in London in 1795, and received his earliest education at a City school, after which he undertook medical studies at Guy's Hospital in Southwark. As he completed these studies, he came into an inheritance which allowed him to establish an independent practice.

This practice, however, was not immediately developed. Responding to a mood more prevalent in those days than now, Dr Cake made a journey to Europe, seeking to acquaint himself with the beauties of the Classical world, but more especially with the discoveries of modern physicians, and with the existing condition of the people. While a visitor to Rome, he became acquainted with members of the English Colony, as it was then called, and in particular with those who expressed support for the overthrow and containment of King Ferdinand, who at that time ruled the twin Kingdoms of Naples and Sicily. Dr Cake did not return to England for a period of several years.

Acquaintances will recollect that Dr Cake attributed his subsequent direction to the sights seen, and beliefs developed, during this travelling time of his life. They were sufficient to ensure that he became a person of unusual dedication. Moving his practice from London to the village of Woodham, where the county of Essex approaches that of Suffolk, he made the countryside his home, and his neighbours the object of his pity and concern. He did not seek a wider reputation – only to publish, occasionally, reports on such findings as his work allowed him to make, and to establish a connection with others who shared his interests.

Dr Cake committed himself to the world, but was a man of retiring habits. He did not marry. In the garden and conservatory of his home, there may be seen the evidence of the one passion which rivalled his affection for his patients – namely, a collection of orchids and other exotic plants. These dumb survivors are a continuing proof of his character, being a sign that all Nature responded to his attention. It has already been proposed that a memorial be raised to his memory, for which donations are invited, and may be sent to the Rector of St Mary's, the Rev. R. L. Phillipps.

Tabor's more intimate account is hand-written, and covers twelve densely packed pages. His script begins as an immaculate, faceless copperplate which soon loses its composure and crouches into a flattened sprint. The first page is headed 'Notes J.C.'s funeral', and the main text is prefaced with a few jottings, as below:

Journey from London – weather – returning to W – funeral – mourners – conversation with AR – visit to house? – return.

For no reason other than to satisfy my own concerns, I shall set down my recollections of the funeral of John

Cake. Perhaps they will be of some use in the future, if ever I undertake the larger work I have in mind – and if not, the labour will have cost me nothing but the passage of a few minutes, and gained me the pleasure of those same minutes in his proximity.

I have written elsewhere of how Dr Cake and I first became acquainted, and I shall not refer now to our subsequent conversations and my suspicions. I shall merely offer the evidence as I found it at the graveside. The service at Woodham was arranged to begin at noon, and I had taken the precaution of leaving my own home in Finchley the previous evening, to lodge at an hotel on the eastern side of the City, from which I could conveniently take a train into Essex. This I did at around nine o'clock in the morning, reaching the small town of Witham after an uneventful journey. I was encumbered only by a suitcase in which I had packed clothes suitable for the occasion, and by my own thoughts.

Skies had been grey when I left London, but as I stepped into a carriage at Witham, and directed the driver to take me across country, sunlight bathed the entire landscape in a gentle warmth. It was a most inapposite day for a funeral, and in particular for such an autumnal soul as Dr Cake. While my conveyance jolted off from the station, it appeared that the town's market was in progress, and the streets (though salubriously broad near the centre) were choked with stalls, and with fellows in from the fields to sell their wares. We were detained for a whole quarter of an hour by a flock of sheep which appeared unusually percipient, and held up traffic as if they meant to delay death itself.

Once we had cleared the town, we came to roads I knew well enough to recognise, but not so well as to find them dulled by familiarity. Approaching Faulkbourne, I noticed the flattened shapes of cottages recently demolished to improve a view from the Hall (a newly-built and monstrous shot at the Elizabethan style, resembling nothing so much as the railway station I had recently departed). A little further on, as we entered Silver End, a mother appeared, wheeling one of her infants in a broken-down hand-cart, on which was also heaped an assortment of clothes, pots, boxes, etc. The exhaustion of her dusty face, and the evidently arduous labour of propelling her vehicle, were both deeply pathetic. No fewer than six other children, in descending order of size, followed in her wake like ducklings waddling behind their parent. I bade my driver to slow down so that I could ask the woman what reason she had for her journey, but he affected not to hear, and we bowled past her so rapidly that until we had gained the next corner and passed out of sight, she was utterly concealed in a muddy cloud.

We then reached an arable area without dwellings of any sort, but with plenty of men and women toiling in the fields. It being still too early for harvest, most of these were patrolling slowly along narrow paths in the wheat, plucking poppies, wild oats, campion flowers, and other rogue elements from the crop. Occasionally the murmur of their talk reached me, and once the notes of a jovial song, but I knew from my experience in the landscape around Finchley that their contentment was an illusion.

When we came to the next few lines of cottages, and saw their mean doorways hanging open onto darkness, their ragged infants playing with sticks and items of rubbish, my heart once again shrank with pity. This sensation was joined by another, of anger, whenever we passed the gateway of some more prosperous property, usually with a pair of griffins, lions, or suchlike, guarding its approach. (I do not, as I have made plain elsewhere, dislike riches for their own sake, merely deplore such differences in situation as still affront us everywhere, even after the passing of the Act.)

And so my journey continued, shaking me between exasperation at our human ways, and pleasure in Nature's balm, until we reached Woodham. Here the oscillations of my mood ceased, and I fell to thinking entirely of the place, and of its late-departed doctor. I was assisted in this by the village's being built on a hill, around the base of which runs the flaggy stream with the threatening name of Blackwater. This hill required my carriage to slow considerably, and the driver to jump down from his seat and walk alongside. We therefore entered Woodham at a funeral pace, with me aloft in my seat, discomforted by my eminence. I now looked over hedges into fields where no one worked – the labourers, I supposed, all preparing to bid their physician farewell. I heard the bees fumbling the weak heads of dog roses that lined the way, and the pony's shoes as it scraped up the incline. To my right, a yellowing expanse made the foreground and the horizon; to my left, a thick belt of elm trees concealed the church, then abruptly ended and left it standing clear: the walls of knapped flint, the modest wooden spire, and the surrounding graveyard generally overgrown. At the sight of this, and at the accompanying sense of the sadness of the occasion, I caught my breath. However deep our acquaintance with death, a fresh encounter always restores an original dismay.

As we reached the brow of the hill and came among the houses I recognised, I was immediately conscious of their silence. Windows stared blindly into the street. Sweet-peas and hollyhocks, which might normally be a subject of conversation among women, or shade for a child, swayed unregarded in the desert air. The sparkling black-and-white fronts of the dwellings – flint-clad, like the church – sullenly returned my gaze. In such a palpable atmosphere of gloom, I considered myself even more conspicuous than before, and urged my driver to continue quickly along the main street to the inn which stood at its end. The horse's hooves now sounded uncommonly loud, and I did not look at anything except my hands, folded in my lap, until I alighted. Then, requesting the driver to wait for me until I should need him again, I went indoors and changed into the more appropriate suit I had brought with me.

On emerging into daylight, severe and solemn as a pillar of basalt, I noticed that the driver had arranged for refreshment to be provided for him and his animal, and I set off back down the silent street to the church. It was a little before noon, and as I stepped carefully through the dust, the bell in the steeple began to toll: a surprisingly deep and satisfying note. As if it had been a signal, the

21

doors of the cottages suddenly disgorged their occupants – dressed in a variety of formal clothes – who joined me in my walk. Few people spoke. All of us proceeded with lowered heads. And before we reached the lych-gate (a pretty red-tiled construction with a kissing gate beside it), a second consequence of the bell became obvious. In the street behind us, and arriving from the direction of Dr Cake's home, appeared a collection of carriages, buggies, and other forms of transport, bearing those from the neighbourhood who could afford such conveyances. Seeing their advance concentrated by the slight upwards tilt of the street, I fancied momentarily that they were a hoard of aggressors, bearing down upon us. The notion faded when I found they were in fact keeping their distance, waiting for us to find our places in the church before they assumed their own. In their midst, and distinguished by a fine plume of black feathers which sprouted above the whole group, was the hearse.

I proceeded as swiftly as was still respectful up the narrow path to the north door. Here I removed my hat and peered ahead. A surprise awaited me. Supposing – in the drama and confusion of the past several minutes – that I was among the first to arrive, I was brought to a dead stop by the prospect of the interior: at least two-thirds of the pews were already full! It was a touching as well as a disconcerting sight. Squeezed into rows (some individuals kneeling, but most sitting in silence) were whole families including their children, sun-browned individuals whom I took by their leathery appearance to be labourers, a sprinkling of more affluent hats: the whole community, in fact, that Dr Cake had served, now united in sorrow at his parting. It disturbed me that, having made such a lengthy journey to be among them, I had no choice except to find a place towards the back of the church, where I would be remote from the proceedings. But no sooner had I admitted this to myself than I appreciated it was only my pride which made me feel such a thing. Accordingly, I made my way forward with a show of willingness (the other late-comers pressing behind and around me) and found a seat by a pillar which partly obscured my view of the choir and altar.

There then followed the entry of the grander personages I had glimpsed in the street a moment before. It was in its way a remarkable sight, but not one which differed in fundamental respects from other such scenes I had observed at home in Finchley. Self-important gentry in the glossy plumage of their mourning; galleon wives floating on waves of black tulle; polished children. Only one detail in the procession struck me as unusual: the sight of Dr Cake's housekeeper, Mrs Reilly, amid the main party as though she were truly a part of it. Notwithstanding the mask of her veil, the extreme pallor of her skin was clearly visible. She appeared intent on acknowledging no one and, gaining her seat, immediately leaned forward and bowed her head so as to block even the side view that I had of her.

The organ all this time performed a meandering kind of melody, its reedy progress through an assortment of minor keys (not all intended) punctuated by the strenuous wheezing of a bellows. Now, at some sign I could not detect, it plunged into a more definite and melancholy direction, whereupon the entire congregation rose and the coffin was borne up the aisle to the crossing, on the shoulders of four red-faced ancients. However frequent is our attendance at funerals, we can never follow the actions of pall-bearers without supposing some accident will befall them, causing them to drop their precious burden. Nor can we see the coffin of a person we have known, without experiencing some new shock of loss. In this respect, a coffin is like a mirror, in which we see the image of our own condition, and understand that our human differences, whether of appearance, morality or wealth, must finally be reconciled.

As these thoughts passed through me, the body of my late acquaintance was laid on a pair of trestles, the bearers made their way into some shadowy recess, and the service began. I shall say nothing of this, since it followed a pattern familiar to all of us. I shall only point out that the Rector – the Rev'd Phillipps, a nervous fellow who seemed to be in perpetual danger of disappearing into the folds and billows of his vestments – spoke with an unexpected vigour when the time came for his address. The rustling of the congregation, and the distraction of their sniffing and coughing, entirely ceased. It was, truth to tell, an ordinary production in itself, yet Dr Cake's qualities were made a matter of such consequence, and his death such a severe deprivation, that the whole gathering could do no more than gaze upon the floor.

When I had composed myself, I fixed my own attention on a representation of our Saviour which appeared in the central panel of the west window. Dr Cake, I knew, doubted His divinity but acknowledged his virtues; now, as the celestial face shone with an intermittent radiance (the sun bustling in and out of cloud in the sky beyond), I felt it possible to accept that the pursuit of human goodness, regardless of any relation to the Almighty, was an adequate achievement in life. As I glanced round at the mourners who were my fellows that day, and saw their tear-filled eyes, I felt that Dr Cake had indeed fulfilled a higher purpose.

The closing hymn, in which the organist was finally overwhelmed by the mysteries of his art, and abandoned the congregation to their own devices, put paid to such elevated thoughts. I detected a similar descent in my neighbour, a tightly-dressed yeoman whose left hand, as it fluttered the pages of the hymnal, displayed an alarming and barely-healed gash through the nail of the thumb. As the tune strayed into inconsequence, he gave an audible groan, such as a man might make at the appearance of a recurring weakness. Emboldened by this show of spirit, I resolved to abandon my hitherto apologetic ways – and when the coffin was carried out of the church for burial, I pressed after it, determined to secure a ring-side position (as it were). This I managed to do, not caring that several of the grander party looked askance at me as I pressed through their ranks.

The grave which had been dug for Dr Cake lay at the northern end of the churchyard, where the land fell away steeply beyond a low brick wall to the Blackwater. A light breeze blew up the slope of the valley, ruffling the stream into a thread of silver, swaying the heads of the corn, and faintly distressing the clothes of all those in attendance. In different circumstances, it would have appeared a simple pastoral scene. Now it seemed pregnant with a sense of change. In the far distance, I heard the strenuous breathing of a railway train. In a yard on the opposite slope (which I guessed must belong to a different parish) I could discern with difficulty a group of men resting in the shade before they were dispatched for their afternoon's labours. All this, combined with the more obvious fact that Dr Cake's death must mean an upheaval in the village, persuaded me that my hilltop view had the effect of freezing time at a precarious moment of penultimacy. Generally we lead our lives helter-skelter, without noticing its individual divisions, so that when we become aware of some difference in our circumstances it surprises us. Today I understood that when Dr Cake had been laid in the earth, and his mourners had scattered, the great iron engine of our century would drive us forward at a distinctly different speed. It was a sombre reflection, as though in bidding farewell to my acquaintance I was also entering a new chamber of existence.

Once again, matters of fact broke into my thoughts and destroyed them. The bearers had now deposited their load on stout oak planks laid across the grave, and as soon as we were all assembled the Rector began his intonation, settling at once into his original nervous and floundering manner. Nevertheless, the beauty of his words held us suspended, so that I gazed upon the coffin-lid in a kind of trance. The sunlight brought out its network of knots and whorls, and the brass handles gleamed with a redundant opulence. The familiarity of these details, and of my responses to them, dulled my mood still further. Indeed, it was only when I leaned forward a little, to look round the obstacle of my neighbour's shoulder, that my reverie ended. The square brass plate, screwed into the coffin-lid near the head, was entirely blank.

I immediately forgot the meaning of the words still tumbling into my ears. The grass beneath my shoes, the breeze pressing against my face, the susurration of a chestnut tree near the lych gate – all these were as nothing. The error was a small thing in itself, yet it shocked me. To travel into the unknown with no name . . . To lie in wait for the resurrection beneath the burden of a mistake . . . Such notions gave me a sharp offence, cutting across every doubt I entertain concerning the whole matter of faith, and converting me for a moment into a true believer. It was not long, however, before I reversed my thoughts. It occurred to me that the blankness was not a mistake but a deliberate intention. It was Dr Cake's final communication with the world – a message sent in his own particular code. I read it inwardly, and understood.

The exhilaration of this contact with the doctor was so great, I felt I had actually reached through the lid of the coffin, touched the body, and discovered it was still warm. Indeed, as the oak struts were replaced with canvas straps, and the weight of the man was lowered out of sight, I believe that I might even have smiled to myself, whilst others were keeping long faces or actually weeping. I was filled with a sense of conviction, which I would share with no one.

This new mood, into which I had so suddenly been translated, made me reluctant to fulfil my original intentions, which were to remain in the village until after the service had been completed, and to attend whatever gathering had been arranged. When the Rector had finished his part, folded his book, and fluttered away towards the lych-gate, I stepped smartly back from the grave, leaving other stricken souls to stare mournfully into its abyss for a moment longer. The muffled but resounding echoes they made, dropping handfuls of earth onto the coffin, haunted me as I found the path that ran alongside the church. Here I slowed my pace, not wishing to give offence by my haste, and glanced meditatively from left to right, hoping to give the impression of a man printing the scene on his memory for future recollection. The Blackwater flashed at me from its reedy bed in the valley. Two grave-diggers, dressed in coarse shirts and with their trousers tied at the ankles, lounged in the shade of the chestnut tree. A collar dove crooned above their heads.

'Dr Tabor?'

It was a woman's voice, spoken softly behind my back. I was for a moment astonished to hear my name, believing myself unknown in the village. But this surprise quickly melted, as I recognised the rolling cadence of Mrs Reilly. She was standing with one foot in front of the other, giving the appearance of movement though actually stock still. Her veil was now pinned to the brim of her hat, showing her pinched face and sore eyes. I immediately shook her hand, indicating that it was not indifference which had made me quit the graveside, but a turbulence of strong emotion.

'I hope you will come back to the house, Sir.' Her voice was firm, and her feet now drawn tidily together.

'Mrs Reilly, please do not think that I . . .'

'There is a ham.'

'That is most kind. But I have a carriage waiting.'

'The doctor would have been disappointed.'

'You are gracious to say so.'

We continued thus for a minute or two, both made awkward by the several differences which divided us. Mrs Reilly wrung her hands as she spoke, sometimes pausing to twist a strand of her red hair away from her mouth. I studied her more closely, noticing the marks of her grief. To my professional eye, it appeared that she was not in good health. Bright spots of colour burned in her cheeks, and her slight frame shivered slightly.

Yet I was as much struck by her nervousness as I was by her fragility. 'Mrs Reilly,' I said, 'is there some difficulty?'

'O no, Sir,' she replied briskly, understanding me to be concerned about her material circumstances. 'The doctor has seen to that. I shall be staying on at the house and shall manage quite well, thank you.'

'Then what . . .?' But my obstinacy (as I now see it must have appeared) defeated her, and made her change direction.

'It is no matter,' she said. 'I may write to you, though, may I not? I have your address. It is the same as before?'

The question was superfluous, since only a few weeks had elapsed since our last meeting. However, I nodded without adding any comment.

'Well, then. Thank you, Sir.' She gave a little bobbing curtsey, and looked round at the crowd of others who were now advancing towards us from the graveside.

'I shall expect to hear from you,' I said decisively. 'And now if you will forgive me I must leave you. I have a long journey.'

For the first and only time in our conversation she then looked me fully in the face, her anxiety replaced by simple earnestness. As she spoke, a finger of breeze stole up the valley and brushed another fiery ringlet of hair across her cheek so that (not for the first time) I glimpsed her as she must have been when a younger woman – beautiful and intense, conscious of herself as one of the millions whose lives have been narrowed by circumstances. There was no trace of bitterness in her expression, only of compassionate sadness. I smiled at her, but her own features remained fixed.

'Perhaps you could do one thing,' she added. 'You could write an appreciation of the doctor. Our newspaper, the *Messenger*, has asked for one and I have already mentioned that I hope you will supply it. I have told them that you knew the doctor better than most.'

I was so utterly taken aback by this, I could do no more than gasp 'But Mrs Reilly! We met on no more than two occasions! I could say only . . .' I did not complete my sentence. Her eyes were levelled on mine as if she were a veritable Ancient Mariner, and had seen through their surfaces and discerned secrets of which I was myself unaware.

'It is the truth, Sir,' she said with an iron finality. 'You knew him better than most.'

Shaken into acquiescence by this, and a little flattered by her insistence, I merely replied: 'Very well then. Please tell them to contact me and I shall do my best.'

She held my gaze for a moment longer, her mouth clamped shut, and I do not believe would have spoken more, even had the other mourners not at that moment joined us. 'Well, well . . . ,' one of them broke in, a rough-faced and burly man who obviously recognised Mrs Reilly, but would not shake her hand. She at once fell into a more deferential manner, and stepped backwards. Seeing that our strange, inexpressive link had been broken, I made my farewells, speaking to the crown of Mrs Reilly's hat. After a polite exchange with the Rector, a quick march up the village street, and a change into my travelling clothes, I climbed aboard my carriage and returned to Witham. Sunlight still poured down, as it had done on the journey out. The driver still cursed or lapsed into silence alternately. His horse still slowed or stirred into a reluctant trot as the gradient demanded. There was nothing in the wide world to show that a great change in Nature had occurred.

Two

In his reminiscence of the funeral, Tabor says he has 'written elsewhere of how Dr Cake and I first became acquainted'. This 'elsewhere' in fact comprises two long documents, both handwritten, the first in a steadier script than the 'Notes', and possibly a fair copy Tabor considered passing to a printer. It is dated 'June –? 1844'. In other words, Tabor began writing immediately after his first visit to Woodham, and two months before Cake's death.

My acquaintance with Dr John Cake of Woodham in the county of Essex has been occasioned by my knowledge of his medical work. While preparing my *Survey*, I have taken it upon myself to complement my findings, and solidify my conclusions, by seeking out various others whose interests coincide with my own. Dr Cake, having produced a number of articles which report on the circumstances of his neighbourhood, was an obvious choice, and I did not hesitate to write to him, even while he was still a stranger to me.

It is not my purpose here to anticipate questions I shall

address in my *Survey*, and it is therefore also not my wish to describe Dr Cake's work in detail. Suffice it to say that he has made the treatment of consumption a particular concern – although on the basis of our conversations today, I should say that whatever relief he brings to his patients is more probably the result of his exceptional nature than any particular remedy. Truly, in all my life, I have seldom encountered a man in whom the spirit of goodness moved to such obvious effect. After so little time as a few hours in his company, I feel confident of this. His is in many respects a superior life, certainly a valuable one. Yet it is also a life which contains mysteries, as I shall suggest, and shall hope to discover more thoroughly.

It has become my habit, while preparing my *Survey*, to record my findings in a regular fashion at the end of each day's work. My encounter with Dr Cake has been so remarkable, I shall depart from the usual catalogue of facts, and give a full account of our meeting. Such an approach will have the advantage of preserving necessary details, and also of securing wider interests – although I anticipate there will be an inevitable sense of compression, even sometimes of brevity, in what I say, since it is not my intention to give a breath-by-breath version of things, rather a sufficient sense of their character for my readers to feel both drama and import.

That being my intention, I will say to my imaginary audience that I am presently installed in an upper room of the Bell, in Dr Cake's village of Woodham, having recently left his house. Rising from the tap-room beneath

34

me are the voices of those who take comfort in its resources, but otherwise there is quiet. If I part my curtains and look into the street, I see nothing to occupy my attention beyond a few house-lights, and the movement of leaves on a large ash-tree which grows in the yard. My room itself is simple and clean: a narrow bed (but hard, as I have already discovered), a dresser on which stands a pitcher and ewer decorated with a faded scene of cattle grazing, and this plain table at which I am presently seated. My candle is contained in a contraption designed for outdoor work, which was passed to me with great ceremony by the landlord when I informed him that I intended to study before sleeping. It is certainly adequate to its task.

Dr Cake had bidden me to arrive at his house in the early part of the afternoon, which I managed to do after a journey from my home to London, then from London to the market town of Witham, from whence a carriage brought me the remaining few miles with much complaining. It is a picturesque road, and passes many good stone houses and well-tended pastures, but also includes sights that are material to my *Survey*. I noticed one whole village which had been moved for the convenience of a great landowner, a number of cottages so meanly appointed that they cannot help but breed sickness, and a quantity of common acres which have been recently enclosed – according to the evidence of new fences.

Woodham is a more fortunate village than many. Dr Cake informed me that the gentleman who inhabits the Hall (which stands adjacent to the church, but is con-

cealed from it by plantations) has a philanthropic manner, and often with his family of daughters makes visits to
the cottages with parcels of food. There is, indeed, a well-
tempered air to the place which compares favourably
with conditions elsewhere in our country, and I dare say
this reflects the care shown by the good doctor. However,
and as he admits himself, this care is not so reliable that it
can altogether withstand the predations of poverty, and
in the Spring just gone by a veritable plague afflicted several of the poorest dwellings. The results may be seen in
the churchyard; in one case an entire family of four children was destroyed, and now lies together in a common
grave. Dr Cake supposes the cause of death to have been
scarlet fever, and I can see no reason to disagree.

But I repeat: it is not my purpose to engage deeply with
professional matters here. Hearing the church clock strike
nine, I am persuaded to end my digression.

I approached Dr Cake's house with no expectations of
how it might appear, since I knew nothing of his material
circumstances. It is a building of some twenty years'
standing, and constructed in the Regency style – which is
to say: symmetrical, and painted white. The effect is to
make one think of a large suburban villa, rather than a
country house, but this is not unpleasing. Seen from the
lane, at the head of its short but serviceable drive, it suggests good taste and a good reputation. There is nothing
ostentatious, though it has an appearance of solidity and
quiet gracefulness. It must be said, this impression is
somewhat compromised by the paintwork of the house
being in need of renewal – there are some distinct green

patches on the walls – and by the outbuildings being generally decayed. The garden is not visible from the front, but there is a field of grazing to one side, close-cropped to give the effect of a miniature park, and on the other a thickly-planted copse of mixed pine, ash, oak and beech.

A housekeeper answered my knock, and when I gave my name, she informed me (in an Irish accent) that the doctor would see me in his study. I did not at this stage pay her any significant attention, but was struck by her implication that if I had been a patient I would have been shown to another room. The hall was very dark, as is often the case with houses of such a tight formal construction; however, when I had left my hat on a table placed for the purpose, she let me through the appointed door, and I was astonished by a deluge of light.

My host was not visible, and I took a moment to look around me. I may say at this point that I have made a habit all my life of encountering each fresh scene of my existence as though I might later be required to remember it exactly – which no doubt has something to do with the responsibilities of my profession. I shall therefore try and render my impressions as though I were producing an *etching*. A large French window gave onto a strip of lawn, an iron railing, and a view of the grazing – over which the shadows of cloud were passing in a stately procession. Restoring my attention to the room, I found that one wall was concealed behind an enormous case of books, rising from floor to ceiling; I did not examine them, since I feared imminent discovery, but I noticed that a remarkable number were not, as I supposed they would be, medical volumes but literary ones: plays and poetry. The remaining walls were covered with paper of a heavy purple and gold pattern, which gave the room, for all its height and airiness, the appearance of a jewel box.

This sense of almost luxurious comfort was intensified by the paintings – or, I should more properly say, the engravings – which were closely assembled and hung in gilded frames. So far as I could tell at a glance, these seemed to show scenes from Classical mythology, and in a few cases Italian city- and landscapes. I had the impression (helter-skelter and in confusion) of massive ruins sprouting vegetation, of collapsed pillars and capitals, of drapery billowing round bare arms and legs. The floor created the same effect of profusion, being covered in smooth-woven carpets, mainly of deep greens and yellows. I say covered, but in truth there was only a little space available for this kind of decoration, since the room was crowded with furniture: a settle in front of the window, a bureau along the facing wall, and a scattering of assorted chairs, stools, occasional tables, and other items. On one of these tables, situated in the dead centre of the window so as to catch the light and spin it across the walls and ceilings at all angles, was a perfectly round bowl of clear water, in which four or five goldfish swam in dreamy circles. The effect was delightful, all the more so since the window was framed with tendrils of japonica and myrtle, growing against the exterior walls of the house.

Such was my pleasure in these sights, I barely noticed the screen placed to conceal the fireplace to my left. Its tall boards – painted a drab green – were decorated with yet more Classical scenes, cut from the pages of magazines and pasted together to make a kaleidoscope of antiquity. From behind this screen, I now discerned the faint rasp of human breath, taken and expelled with difficulty. Looking behind me, I found the housekeeper had silently departed, closing the door behind her, and understood that I must introduce myself.

'Dr Cake?' My words seemed unnaturally thin, being absorbed by the furnishings etc around me. There was a little gasp, half of surprise, half of impatience, and a voice deeper than my own replied:

'Come forward.'

I did as I was instructed, winding round the edge of the screen and coming to a halt once again. Dr Cake lay on a faded lime coloured chaise, smiling up at me and extending his right hand as though he expected me to kiss it. I did not do so, but felt perplexed enough by the strangeness of his greeting to unravel a string of platitudes. 'It is good of you to see me, Sir, knowing the demands that others make on your time' – or some such nothing. At this Dr Cake lowered his hand, whereupon I leaned forward and shook it gently. There was a clamminess about it, a mixture of hot and cold, which confirmed the impression I had already received. The doctor was a sick man; possibly even a dying man.

I sat on a low chair upholstered in brown tapestry, which had been placed at his elbow, and we regarded each other in silence. I cannot tell what idea he gained of me, only that he studied my face with a serene steadiness, as if no barrier existed between us. It was a look of the utmost candour and simplicity. My sense of him, on the contrary, was distinct. Indeed, I believe I shall never forget that original meeting and contact, such was its power. Even though obviously unwell, he was dressed to go out, in an old-fashioned worsted suit with no waistcoat, and a high-collared shirt. A fawn blanket was drawn up to his waist, making it difficult for me to gain an accurate notion of his height, but I gained the impression (later confirmed) that he was an unusually small man. The hands – now folded across his stomach – were delicate and fine-boned, the shoulders narrow, and the neck as pale-skinned as a girl's might be if she kept herself from the sun. His head, too, was delicate, and being almost hairless, save for a kind of tonsure, which must once have been reddish but was now salt-and-pepper, reminded me of a young bird which has toppled from its nest. The deep blue eyes were widely-spaced, the nose was arched, and the mouth – exceptionally wide – had the distinction of a top lip which slightly over-hung the lower and fuller one. It gave an appearance of eagerness, almost of panting and pursuit, which not even the weariness of his body could obliterate.

Was this the face of a medical man, I asked myself? The creases on the brow, and beside the eyes, suggested an impressive knowledge of suffering. Yet the alabaster skin, the bright directness of the gaze, the (once again) exceptional mouth, all bespoke a temperament I could only conceive as artistic. Dr Cake seemed suspended between languor and enthusiasm – someone who expressed a deep curiosity about this world, yet at the same time looked beyond its material boundaries.

'Truly, sir,' I said, beginning my platitudes once again, 'it is most kind of you . . .'

'The kindness is yours in making so troublesome a journey,' he said, in a deep sing-song, which combined the strange jaggedness and flatness we find in Londoners. He glanced down, surveying his own weakened shape, then continued. 'I am not as I was, and therefore cannot report precisely on the situation as it exists here, to help you with your work. There is another man in the village, a Dr Garrett, who now sees the majority of my patients. I can give you an introduction if you wish.'

I was a little disappointed at this, and wondered why the doctor had invited me since he felt as he did. I think I may have leaned back a little in my chair, perhaps, deliberating how to proceed. At any rate, it was now that I began to notice the furnishings in this part of the room, which had previously been hidden by the screen. Behind me, and warming my back with a pleasant glow, was a wood fire in a wide grate, and on the mantel above it a miniature grandfather clock known I believe as a grand-*mother*. Above this, and therefore pitched at an uncomfortable height on the wall, but obviously determined to occupy the pride of place was — . I had expected a family portrait, perhaps, or an especially beloved scene. In fact it was the familiar engraving of Shakespeare by Droeshout, which appears in many editions of the Bard's works, curiously decorated with a small swag of cloth, from which depended two silk tassels.

I glanced away from this – for no reason except surprise – and completed my inspection. The engravings in the main part of the room were here supplanted by images depicting scenes from Shakespeare's plays: Romeo, for instance, addressing Juliet on her balcony. There was also another small case of books, a bronze statuette of Bonaparte, and a neat upright desk (closed) on which was placed an Aeolian harp, quite silent. In the furthest corner from Dr Cake, but exactly in his line of sight, was a green linnet in a cage. This was a most beautiful and delicate creature, in some parts of its plumage as bright as an emerald, in others a pale yellow. It was regarding my inspection of the room, I noticed, with one eye closed and the other open, tilting its head to one side as it did so.

As I say, my first impression of the room had been that it resembled a jewel box. In this sequestered part it seemed a veritable treasure trove – the relics and knick-knacks of an entire life heaped together. I turned to Shakespeare again, gazing down in his seniority, and as I did so became conscious that my curiosity must appear vulgar. When I faced Dr Cake I found that he was smiling (which, incidentally, allowed me to see that he retained a good many of his teeth).

'You are surprised to see him here?' he said, without taking his eyes from me.

'A little.'

'But you are a literary man yourself.'

I was frankly astonished at this, and fell silent. It was many years since I had considered myself such a thing, and my reputation in that respect was such that I did not expect to hear it mentioned in so remote a place as Woodham. In Finchley it is a different matter. Although my duties are those of a doctor, they have never prevented me from expressing a sympathetic interest in literature in general, and in poetry especially. Indeed, I have been fortunate enough to discover a sufficient number of enthusiasts to form a small Society, which meets to discuss such things. At no time, however, have I felt able to make contributions of my own, since I consider my verses to have been the product of the particular circumstances of my youth. But my idols of those early days – the Lake poets and their descendants the Cockney School – have remained (as it were) my guiding lights, and I readily accept that their expressions of humanity will prove as valuable to society as the wisdom of scientific men. Wordsworth, in particular, and his sometime-acolyte John Keats, may truly be called physicians of the soul.

Dr Cake maintained the steady beam of his attention, a smile still playing about his mouth.

'I am one of those,' I said, with what I hoped was enough dignity to conceal my astonishment, 'on whom the Muses have sprinkled their gifts – no more.'

'Come, come,' said the doctor, with an alacrity which made my apology seem not modest – as I had intended – but proud. 'I have read your book. I have a copy on my shelves. It has some fine things. Any man who admires Wordsworth must himself be admirable in some degree.'

The simple friendliness of this enabled me to speak more freely. 'Your implication that I was of Wordsworth's school is of course true. I was young when I wrote, and easily influenced.'

'Wordsworth was young when he wrote.'

43

'Wordsworth had genius.'

'Also true, though even his most ardent supporters agree that his genius left him.'

The smile faded, and Dr Cake unfolded his hands, looking solemnly into his open palms, as though he meant to discover there the story of his own future. 'This is in the nature of things. Such works as we create are not entirely within our power; they depend on mysterious agencies, which linger or depart as they think fit, and not as we demand.'

'Do you speak of yourself, Dr Cake?' As I put the question, I did not entirely understand what I meant – only that he had spoken with an urgency which suggested some personal interest.

He paused, without looking up, then said, 'I will not speak of myself for the moment, except to answer those questions you have for me. But I think you may see by looking around you that my pursuits have not been entirely medical.'

'I see Shakespeare, of course.'

'Shakespeare is our great presider.'

'No doubt.'

'I am glad to hear you say that.' He folded his hands again, and when I consider that modest action now, in the tranquillity of recollection, I understand something I did not then fully comprehend. In speaking about poetry and its fluctuations of power, the doctor had brought himself to the threshold of some larger and more expressive utterance – from which he withdrew immediately. To recover himself, he changed the conversation suddenly

44

into a new and more solemn direction.

'I noticed you observing our little song bird,' he said, his eyes brightening towards the linnet in her cage.

'It is a most charming specimen,' I replied, 'but I have yet to hear her sing.'

'She will sing in due course,' said the doctor, still twinkling. 'I have named her Polly.'

'But that is a parrot's name,' I expostulated, feeling that I was trampling heavily where the joke required me to be nimble.

The doctor's smile faded and he did not answer me directly. 'She is a beautiful creature,' he said wistfully. 'Sweet-natured.'

'How can you tell that?'

'She is always cheerful. I can rely on her for that, and other kinds of delight.'

I hesitated at this, uncertain how best to continue, whereupon the doctor abruptly switched direction again, back to my own case.

'Do you mean that the volume you have published contains all that you have written, or that you have ceased publication?'

As he spoke the last word, the linnet, seeming to have absorbed the fact that she had been the subject of our discussion, stirred in her cage and issued a few notes of song. It was a pretty sound but to my ears unsettling in the closeness of the room, suggesting more an idea of imprisonment than anything. 'I have a few things,' I said reluctantly. 'Odds and ends. It is a brave man who publishes – braver than the world knows.'

The doctor was holding up one hand, palm outwards, gazing at the bird while waiting for her notes to fade. In a while he continued our conversation by asking: 'In what respect?'

I shrugged. 'I am speaking hypothetically. As I say, I no longer consider myself a poet. When I spoke of bravery, I meant the willingness to submit in public . . .'

Dr Cake interrupted me with a single word. 'Reviewers.' A new note jarred his voice, and his face darkened so bloodily I almost feared for his health. Then, lifting his head urgently from the chaise until it was inches from my face, he continued: 'They are devils. Devils. I have seen good men, good authors, broken by their deprecations. The worst of it is their presumption in supposing that those they chastise do not know their own faults, and admonish themselves with a ferocity others can only imagine. To berate an author is merely to add injury to insult.'

He ceased, but continued leaning forward a moment, so that I caught the odour of decay which came from his mouth. Then he sank back. When his face cleared again, I was struck as if for the first time by the quality of his natural expression. It had a serenity which made him appear truly angelic. I felt it incumbent on me to calm him further.

'My own publications received such little attention,' I said mildly, 'I cannot consider myself properly criticised.'

'Neglect is a different form of injury,' replied the doctor, but without his former warmth. 'However. We must leave all the significant measuring of success or failure to those who come after us, do you not agree? Posterity is our only judge.'

I nodded at this, and entertained a picture of my book bobbing on the waters of my earlier life, like a small boat far out to sea. 'I hardly think that posterity will concern itself with me. Or with my poetical compositions at any rate. They were a product of my youth, as I say; I have since devoted myself to practical matters.'

Once again, the doctor hesitated as though unwilling to recognise the proper reason for our meeting. 'Yes,' he said eventually. 'We should speak of such things.' Then he twinkled, reaching for a small silver bell I had not previously noticed, which lay partly concealed by his blanket, and shaking it hard. 'But first a glass of claret. Mrs Reilly will fetch it.'

As the ring of the bell still lingered, the door opened and the housekeeper appeared, bearing a decanter and two glasses on a wooden tray. When she had set them down beside us, she folded back one section of the screen, opening a view of the French window, and beyond that of the level green field.

'You will look at my garden before you go?' enquired the doctor. 'It is behind the house; you cannot see it from here. He should see our treasures should he not, Mrs Reilly?'

The housekeeper was now standing at the foot of the chaise, her hands clasped quietly in front of her. As I have said, I had not taken the opportunity to regard her closely when I had entered, being so anxious to speak directly with Dr Cake. Now I saw that she was a slender woman in her forties, with curls of the most radiant redness escaping from beneath her cap. Her skin (as is often the case with red-heads) was of an exceptional milky transparency, which would have matched the doctor's for pallor, had it not been liberally strewn with freckles. I should have called her a striking woman, rather than a beautiful one: there was a crouching quality about her which suggested a cat poised to leap on its prey. Polly, as I now familiarly called the linnet to myself, ruffled and re-arranged her wings with a distinct little whirring noise as Mrs Reilly awaited her next instructions.

'Will that be all, Sir?' she asked the doctor, looking at him fiercely. I had supposed there might be some tension between them, relating to a matter of which I knew nothing. Now I understood that she was protecting him, and silently enquiring whether she should extract me from the room.

'Nothing more,' came the level answer. 'Dr Tabor and I were discussing the poets and their fates.' At this Mrs Reilly boggled a little, then turned on her heel and left us. The doctor waited a moment then added in a low voice: 'Mrs Reilly is a most interesting woman. Her family are Catholics and have therefore been stirred up in ways you might expect. some of them are agitators, I believe – Ribbonmen or some such – and she is in England to escape the persecution endured by others of her acquaintance. Poor woman, her husband died – of consumption, she tells me. I have taken her in. She is in low spirits at the moment, I regret, owing to the situation in her native country.'

'The hunger, you mean.'

'The famine, exactly.' The doctor pointed to the wine, inviting me to fill the glasses for him. As I did so, he asked, 'Have you visited Ireland at all, Dr Tabor?' I shook my head, passing him a glass which he lifted towards the window, narrowing his eyes and peering through the liquid as though it were coloured glass. 'A tragic island,' he said. 'In my own youth I visited for no good reason beyond seeing what beauties it had to offer, yet all I found were scenes of sorrow. Miseries I shall never forget.'

With this he hoisted the glass in my direction and said with solemn authority: 'To the Immortal Spirit', whereupon we both drank. I noticed that the doctor did not immediately swallow, but rolled the wine around his mouth, luxuriating in its taste before letting it vanish down his throat in trickles. When this performance was finished he sighed, smiling with a boyish eagerness. 'It is delicious, is it not, to continue with such pleasures even amidst suffering. We are fortunate creatures.'

I said nothing, debating inwardly with myself. I had not been in the company of Dr Cake for more than half an hour, yet already I felt strongly affected by his personality. This was in part due to his being so unlike the person I had expected. The articles I had read, the bustle of their engagement with the world, had led me to anticipate a very active and practical man. The one who lay before me, notwithstanding the evidence of his illness, was a sensualist. But it was not only the contrast between my anticipation and the reality which impressed me. It was – how shall I put this? It was the sense of his life within the world. He seemed hidden, content with obscurity, yet at the same time linked to larger issues and longer stretches of time. In a nutshell, he appeared more than himself – and willing to share that largeness of spirit immediately with one who had come to him as a stranger.

I drained my glass in two swift mouthfuls as is my habit (to which the doctor did not seem to object), and as its fumes rose into my brain, filling the spaces between my loose thoughts, and inspiring me with a confidence I welcomed, I said: 'Perhaps you would tell me something of yourself, Sir, as a background to the work you have done.'

Dr Cake waved his hand towards the decanter, inviting me to re-charge our glasses. As I did so I noticed, irrelevantly, the sun roll a shadow across the wall behind him in the shape of a horse. It grazed, reared upon its hind legs, pawed the air, and then evaporated, all in the space of a few seconds. The doctor brought me back to myself, clearing the phlegm from his throat.

'My story is simply told,' he said. 'The circumstances of my childhood made it inevitable that I should enter the profession which has since become my life. But I confess there were some uncertainties and indirections.'

'You mean?'

'It would be tedious to relate. But I will admit to you that my studies were interrupted by an illness which required me to travel abroad as a young man.'

'Dr Cake,' I interrupted. 'I did not mean to trouble you for a whole review.'

'No matter,' he said, swaying his head gently from side

to side. 'I will also admit that I protested bitterly against my condition. It is the privilege of youth, is it not, to feel that it should be extended, and develop into maturity. Today I feel differently. It is inevitable that we should die.' Now he moved his free hand onto his chest and let it lie there, the fingers poked inside the folds of his shirt to touch his skin. 'I have seen enough to know what must happen to me. I accept it. It is not a source of grief to me, and there are few enough to elevate my disappearance into a matter of significance. Mine has been a solitary life. A busy one, certainly, and surrounded by others, but a solitary one for all that.'

I could think of no adequate response to these remarks, which I found shocking in their simplicity, and so hung my head and let the doctor continue. I realised that small blades of grass were adhering to the toes of my boots, which I must have collected on my walk to the house, and hoped I had not trampled into the hall on my way through.

'Yes,' the doctor said. 'I was away from London for several years – I should have explained: London was my original home. For the first part of this time I was recuperating, and did very little. But when the sunnier climates had worked their effect, as mercifully they managed to do, I felt compelled to make the most of my exile, and therefore delayed my return.'

'Not exile?' I replied quickly, lifting my head again.

'I considered it such. Mine was not a wealthy family, and those of us whom fortune spared were all of one mind in considering ourselves oppressed by the burden of society. We scattered accordingly. For my own part, I was relieved to find some means of cancelling my first try at life, and of beginning it again.'

'That is not possible.' I spoke with more conviction than good manners should have allowed, and was aware of blushing, but this did not perturb the doctor. With his head still reclining backwards, and speaking as though he were addressing the audience of dust-motes which filtered through the sunlit air, he merely assented.

'You are quite right. It is why we are meeting today. Although we may suppose there are certain chambers in our existence, through which we move if we are spared to do so, acquiring greater degrees of knowledge and so forth as our experience allows, yet we also maintain certain loyalties and interests that Nature gave us at our birth. I have said that my original circumstances required me to leave England while still a young man, and it is true that my condition was a source of anxiety to myself and others.' Here the doctor paused, and his face darkened again, not with anger as before, but with pain.

'Anxiety of what sort?' I enquired gently, reluctant to press him on matters so obviously painful. He pursed his lips so that I saw the line of his teeth through his skin, and then relaxed with a petulant sucking noise.

'Anxieties,' he repeated softly. 'But grave ones – though I have no wish to summon your sympathy for a time so long gone by. Anxieties about every aspect of my circumstances.'

'I am sorry to hear it,' I said, still meekly.

The doctor gave a low hum, as though debating with

himself whether or not to expand on his remarks. In that interval I had a startling glimpse of hardship – of poverty, the loss of friends, of the fear of death itself – that came from nowhere, yet was for a moment compelling. I sympathised with the doctor intensely; all the more so, in fact, for knowing his circumstances so vaguely.

At length the doctor ended his reverie, and with what I was beginning to interpret as his customary courage, banished his dark thoughts with a wave of his hand, and looked at me brightly.

'Even the most thunderous clouds have silver linings, and eventually what had oppressed me became the means by which I recovered myself. My health improved. I saw the beauties of the Classical world, which previously had been no more than dreams and stories.'

'You mean you were in Italy?' I said, relieved that we were once again on an even keel.

'In Rome,' the doctor replied, keeping to my new brisk pace. 'The English Colony made me one of their number, and I lived a full life.'

'But what did you do for work?'

The doctor tilted his head towards me, then away. 'For money? A large part of my difficulties at home had depended on the obscurities of the will of a relative, which should have provided me with a modest income. This had become lost in the maze of Chancery, and I had despaired of regaining it. At length, however, and thanks in large part to the good offices of a brother I had, the complications were resolved. I became the beneficiary of a small income which allowed me to live as I wished.'

'Why did you not return straight home again?'

So long a silence followed this question, which I admit might have seemed impertinent, that I almost believed the doctor had not heard me. I became aware of other noises in the house, which were nothing to do with our conversation or our interests, yet seemed a part of them. From the direction of what I took to be the kitchen there came the silver splatter of water falling onto stone; elsewhere the creak of a floor-board, or the whisper of a morsel of masonry falling inside a wall, made the house feel like a living thing, journeying through or responding to the day as though it were a creature not unlike ourselves.

'I had an interest in politics,' he said at length, in a drowsy sort of voice, as though he had been dozing with his eyes open. 'I could not help but feel that the same conditions which oppressed me were also a constraint to others, and I was determined to intervene on their behalf as I had acted on my own. Why else should we devote our lives to medicine, Dr Tabor?'

It was a question to which no answer was expected. The doctor took another, less elaborate drink from his glass, as though to confirm that he was indeed now fully awake again, and continued. 'Long before I travelled to Italy, I knew from our own newspapers of the difficulties that liberal-minded men were experiencing in certain parts of that country, and among the English Colony I learned much more of such matters. Indeed, I became a confirmed sympathiser. Bonaparte' – here his eyes switched to the bronze figure keeping his peace in our midst – 'Bonaparte as you will recall had left the various states of Europe in a ferment.'

At this point I felt compelled to remind Dr Cake that my comparative youth meant what had been living history to him was to me a kind of confused dream, such as all children have before they gain a true perspective on the world. I did not say this with pride, but merely to confirm the difference in our situations.

'I forget,' the doctor replied considerately. 'My own youth is still so vivid, I make the mistake of assuming that my experience must be general. Besides, we need not exhaust ourselves with a reminiscence of that time. I wished to do no more than explain why I did not return more speedily to England. I shall only add that I consorted with various idealists in the kingdoms of Sicily and Naples, in the belief that I could contribute to the public good. When my work had run its course, I left them to their own devices and sailed for London.'

As the doctor finished speaking he set down his glass, using the base to fidget a clear patch among the books, etc, at his elbow. I should have leaned forward to help him, but for the powerful far-away sensation that had come over me while he was speaking. I felt as if his reminiscence of Italy had transported me there myself, and that I too had burst into the wide bay of Naples (which I had seen often in paintings by Turner and others, but never in fact), had watched the smoke pluming from the summit of Mount Vesuvius, had seen the serene terraces of the city, and the innumerable domes, steeples and pinnacles of its important buildings all bathed in golden light. Such was the doctor's power: to suggest by the merest phrase something magical in the world and in himself.

When I composed myself again, he was regarding me intently, and ready to change the subject. 'We have seen such things in our daily work, have we not, Dr Tabor? We have sought out the scenes of suffering which the majority of men deliberately avoid. Yet before I quitted Italy, I experienced sorrows the like of which I have not witnessed since. Men wounded in war. The bitterness of family to family. Heartlessness. I felt these scenes enter into me, and I dare say they changed me. Or confirmed something that already existed. You see why I am telling you this?'

I was a little surprised by the question, since the intensity of the doctor's speech had struck me so powerfully, it had pushed me a little off-balance. I replied stumblingly.

'I suppose because it has become a kind of background to your work in England?'

'Precisely so,' he drove on. 'It has been like a continual engine and inspiration. Or perhaps I should say like a philosopher's stone, which turned such thoughts I once had about our profession from their original innocence into a real and solid conviction. When I set foot on our island once again, I was entirely resolved for medicine. I completed the training I had broken off, and purchased a practice with such funds as I still retained – in London first, but only briefly, and afterwards here.' The doctor paused, then added in a smaller voice, 'I put away my other interests.'

'You have not spoken of these,' I said, hoping to show that my mood kept pace with his, but in fact seeming to display an unwarrantable casualness.

'They do not concern us today,' said Dr Cake forgivingly, in his same quiet tone. 'They belong to the vanished part of my existence.'

Another slight pause followed, and I had the chance to take stock of the subjects we had covered so far, and the experiences we had enjoyed. All the while the doctor had been speaking, I had listened with a fixed concentration. Yet at the same time a part of my mind had broken off, as though it were beyond my control, comparing the matter of his conversation with the surroundings in which I found myself. The density and depth of decorations in the room; the subjects of the engravings; the volumes in the cabinets; the bald and expressionless face of Shakespeare regarding us: these appeared to contradict what Dr Cake had told me. They were, apparently, the expressions of an interest remote from healing. Except they were not remote – on this the doctor and I had already agreed. They were linked by their power to work a salubrious effect. They were both a part of the joint kingdom of Apollo.

'You mean your other writings,' I said at last and gently.

'I have said nothing about other writings.' He turned away my question by speaking in a completely flat tone. The linnet, I noticed, suddenly shook her wings again, making a noise that sounded strangely like her own name: Polly.

'But your room –' I raised one hand and made a flourish, at which the bird fell silent again. 'Anyone may see that . . .'

'I have said nothing about other writings,' the doctor repeated sharply, so that I saw I had angered him and was embarrassed. I was about to apologise, and certainly was beginning to feel the first pricks of self-reproach, when he pre-empted me – whether from the wish to show my regret was unnecessary, or as a further sign of irritation, I cannot tell. His legs gave one or two abrupt kicks, and at the same time he peeled back the blanket which covered him. With a deplorable show of unfeeling curiosity, I observed that he was wearing a pair of delicate light-weight shoes, a little like dancing pumps. Then he bent forward, reddening as he levered himself.

'Perhaps you would like a sight of our garden now?' He eyed the miniature clock as he spoke, which lacked a little of six. I was still unsure whether he blamed me for the spark of anger he had just felt, but was determined in any case that it should not ignite a more general conflagration, and therefore adopted an ameliorative tone.

'I believe I have tired you already,' I said, getting to my feet and offering a hand.

The doctor was immediately softness itself, whereupon I decided that my recent confusion had been unnecessary. It was not my crassness that had disturbed him, but some disappointment he had suffered in himself. It was now his turn to seem accommodating.

'We have not spoken enough of the matters you came to discuss,' he said. 'I must tell you of my work in the village.' He was sitting on the edge of the chaise, shoulders sloped, knees and feet drawn neatly together. It was now that I noticed for the first time (having previously been prevented by the blanket) his remarkable shortness – barely more than five feet tall, with a little round stomach. His face and throat were still flushed by his recent exertion, so that he resembled a robin.

'No, no,' he said, more decisively still. 'It will do me good. You can assist me, and we shall talk as we go.' At this he laid his right hand upon my arm (I felt the pressure of his fingers distinctly through the material of my sleeve) and pulled himself upright. Once again, I caught the deathly scent of him.

'You must forgive me if I forget myself and begin a rhodomontade now and again,' he said, turning to look me directly in the face. On both cheeks, I noticed that blood vessels had broken, which gave his skin the appearance of paper, scribbled over by a tiny hand. He sighed and went on, 'My hot temper was always a weakness of mine. Come, I shall lean on you.'

As soon as he had said this, and we were beginning to shuffle from behind the screen into the brighter light of the room, the door opened and Mrs Reilly entered. I believe that she must have listened to our whole conversation, since the ferocity of her expression was now perfectly evident. She glared at me.

'I have already offered to leave,' I said immediately, like a chastened boy.

'And I have told Dr Tabor he must stay,' said the doctor with a corresponding firmness. 'I have not yet said all that I wish to say. We are to continue our conversation outside and in the fresh air. Will you join us?' He swivelled his head, which made him appear even more exactly like a small bird. But it was not the slight comedy of his gesture which struck me most strongly. It was the fact that he spoke to Mrs Reilly as though he had offended her by accepting help from anyone but herself. I looked silently from one to the other, and felt the force of their difference as it was expressed in their dress, and in the contrast between the doctor's frailty and Mrs Reilly's stubborn health. Yet I also felt a complicity between them, a simple but strong bond, which persuaded me that the house-keeper knew more about her master than was commonly the case. His conversation with me had been crammed with allusions and tantalising summaries. Without any hard proof or evidence, I felt convinced that Mrs Reilly knew the whole landscape of his mind.

'Please,' I said. 'I would enjoy hearing what you have to say.' I regretted my words immediately, fearing that she would interpret them as a condescension. But she did not.

'Thank you, Sir, I will,' was her only reply, given in her characteristic rolling voice, whereupon she stepped between Dr Cake and myself, compelling him to release me and grasp her arm instead. Walking at a respectful distance behind them, as though I were now the menial, I followed them into the dark hall, where I collected my hat, and then slipped through the front door into the yellow evening.

As we passed the window of the doctor's study, I looked in at the scene of our conversation. The goldfish glowed in their bowl of water, still pursuing their slow rotations, and from the darker part of the room I heard the linnet once more, singing in the shadows. The fancy occurred to me that it might have learned everything we said, and be repeating it, as a parrot might indeed be able to do. It was impossible, I knew, and yet it was perhaps at this moment that I decided to preserve everything I could recollect of the doctor's speech. If so, it did not strike me as a conscious decision. I was entirely occupied by the prospect of the empty and silent room, in which every decoration and item of furniture appeared to brood on its own existence. It was a scene which utterly excluded me, and seemed to deny that I had ever sat there, listening and talking. Or rather, one that already declared the doctor to be a ghost, and my own self as well.

The doctor and Mrs Reilly had meanwhile continued their slow progress into the garden, and had reached the edge of a flower-bed which ran along the edge of the grazing (but protected from it by the iron rail). As I joined them, I discovered our narrow path here spread into a wide lawn, rather in the way a stream sometimes bulges into a lake. Opposite me stood an immense evergreen bush (or several bushes grown together) with an entrance cut in the centre, through which one might pass into the gloomy interior, and enjoy the sensation of being in a bower, or hide-away. Further off, at a distance of some two hundred yards across the mown ground, the grass roughened towards an orchard – three rows of apple trees, and three of plums. Their swelling fruit, as yet too small and bitter to be picked, hung in the sunlight like unnecessary lamps. Elsewhere a tall ash tree gave some shade, and a glass-house slouched against the red-brick wall of an adjoining barn. Its door stood open to allow some circulation of the air, and I could dimly discern what appeared to be a line of exotic plants upon a shelf. In the failing light, and in the mist of my ignorance regarding such matters as house-plants, I hazarded a guess that they were orchids.

I was so consumed by the novelty of all this, I did not look for any further significance. But even with such little hindsight as now exists, I see the doctor was offering me something he considered a privilege – a mixture of wild beauty and orderliness which suggested the workings of his own mind. In this respect, the effect of the garden was similar to that of his study. But on this larger scale, and beneath the canopy of the empty sky, its force was at once greater and more subtle. The doctor is a man whose acquaintance with suffering had made him value beauty not as its opposite, but as a component. He is, as I say, a man who looks beyond the limits of the world, even as he gazes steadily upon them.

My silence gradually became an embarrassment to me, and I moved to join him and Mrs Reilly where they stood in shadow beneath the ash tree. As I stopped beside them, they drew a little further apart, though the doctor's hand was still drawn through Mrs Reilly's arm. 'You grow orchids, Sir,' I said, indicating the glass-house.

'It is a hobby of mine,' he replied, with a glow of passion in his voice. 'I do not enjoy them so much in the house as outside. Indoors they oppress me.'

'Oppress you?' I echoed.

With their beauty. It is too intense. Too . . .' He moved his hand from the arm of his companion and twiddled his fingers. 'Too exotic. It suffocates me.' As he finished speaking his hand slid quickly back into its old support.

I nodded as though in agreement, while in truth thinking it extraordinary that he should go to such lengths to produce something he saw so little.

'Besides,' he continued, 'they are a talking point for my patients. On occasion I will bring visitors to inspect them. The sight gives them pleasure.'

I waited for Mrs Reilly to make a comment, but none was forthcoming: she continued staring over the garden with an enigmatic half-smile twisting her mouth a little. The white of her collar shone with a surprising hard clarity. 'It is hardly a cure,' I said in due course, with more severity than I intended.

'No,' he agreed, undeterred. 'But the whole burden of my writings, as you are aware, has been to remind those afflicted by illness of their continuing humanity.'

'I applaud your efforts, you know that.'

'As I have just expressed it, it seems a very little thing. It is so obvious. And yet when you compare such an approach with that of the assorted butchers who form a part of our profession . . .' His voice dwindled, and he leaned more heavily on Mrs Reilly, who seemed on the point of encircling his shoulders in a sideways embrace. 'It was Astley Cooper who set me on my course,' he added, staring at the ground as if peering into the past itself, 'when he was my Senior Surgeon.'

All the flickerings of resentment I had been feel-
during the past few minutes were banished by the soun
of this name. 'I have heard of him, of course!' I exclaimed.
'A wonderful physician, and a great philanthropic soul.'
The warmth of my response was genuine: I felt a real
pleasure in this reference to Cooper, thinking it might
prove a bond of sympathy. But the doctor showed no
special surprise, which gave me the strange conviction
that he already knew my whole story, and had already settled his views on its various facets and ingredients. It persuaded me that I was in some profound sense inferior to
him, or at least junior in quality, as well as years.

'So far as I am aware,' he said calmly, 'Sir Astley had no
peer as a surgeon. Such courage – and such delicacy!'
Then he looked up at last, his face round with wonder,
and his mouth making its typical moist gape. 'You know
he was in France originally.'

'I did. In Paris.'

'Yes, in Paris. Before he became a senior surgeon. He
consorted with the free spirits of the Revolution. I believe
he attended the dying in the Tuileries Gardens on one
occasion.'

His remark found a place in my mind beside his earlier
reminiscence of his own time in Italy, and made a connection. I saw that however retired his life had become in
Woodham, it still fed on these early experiences of the
world, and had not forgotten their lessons. I resolved
once again to address him boldly.

'Why did you not settle in London or some other city
when you returned to England?' The question seemed flat

the strangeness of its setting, but I did not feel disturbed by this. I felt I had the doctor at a slight disadvantage, and was therefore likely to gain some extra
knowledge of him, which I was determined to possess.

'I did, for a little while,' he said, still staring at nothing I
could see. 'But then I came away here. You are asking,
however, why I eventually hid myself?'

'I did not say hide. I know how occupied you have been
here. Your writings prove it.'

'Why then, Dr Tabor, you have answered your own
question. Illness does not respect seclusion, and may be
found everywhere. Youth may grow thin anywhere, and
need our services. I do not think . . .'

At this the doctor broke off, his whole expression altering with a frightening suddenness. I had known that I
would not be allowed to stand indefinitely with him and
Mrs Reilly, and yet I had equally not expected our time to
end so soon. In the swelling eagerness of my pursuit of
the doctor, and in the fascination of his story, I had forgotten the reality of his situation. Now, as I moved to
stand directly in front of him, I saw his eyes begin to stand
out in their sockets, his head jolt forward, and his free
hand fumble at the pocket of his trousers. In a moment –
which seemed an eternity – he produced a large handkerchief which he pressed hard across his mouth. Mrs Reilly
then immediately released his arm and took him by the
shoulders, so that his head rested on her bosom.

'I must ask you to leave us, Dr Tabor.' She spoke rapidly and without looking at me. 'You will understand that I
cannot show you the way, but you will easily find it.'

I barely listened to her, being so agitated by the scene unfolding before me. Hideous big convulsions now shook the doctor, bending him almost double, so that I thought he must be in the act of vomiting. I soon corrected myself. With his handkerchief still smothering his mouth, and his eyes streaming tears, he was coughing. But these were not the coughs of a man who suffers a common cold; they were the unmistakable deep self-lacerations of the consumptive. Even as I watched, spots of blood soaked through his handkerchief. I fancied that they were unnaturally bright, but this was a trick of knowledge, since in that moment I could not properly tell what was bright and what was dark.

'You forget, Mrs Reilly,' I said, with as much authority as seemed decent. 'I am a doctor, not a patient. I shall help you.'

She did not resist this with a speech, only glancing at me across the now almost collapsed body of Dr Cake, and biting her lip. Then, with a quick dip of her own head, as though she had made a decision and was determined to act upon it, she said: 'Very well.'

I saw what I must do. My meeting with the doctor had begun with us both feeling bound by laws at once sociable yet formal. Now a more professional approach was necessary, yet one which also required a kind of intimacy. As Mrs Reilly disengaged the doctor's hands from her own, I slipped my left arm beneath his shoulders, my right behind his knees, and lifted him off his feet. I am a taller man than he was, as I have already noticed, but not an especially strong one, and expected to experience ne difficulty with my load. In fact the doctor seemed astonishingly light, so that I fairly strode towards the front door of his house, as though I were carrying the frail model of a man and not a man himself. Mrs Reilly fluttered beside and before me as we went, occasionally touching the doctor on his arm and head, murmuring soft meaningless sounds. He for his part was entirely silent, no longer coughing, but leaning his head meekly against my neck. I felt the heat of his skin, and the bird-like delicacy of his bones. I heard, or thought I heard, the pounding of his heart, though it may very possibly have been my own.

As we entered the hallway, Mrs Reilly darted ahead, bidding me to follow, and turning up a stairway I had not previously noticed. As we reached the corridor, my burden stirred softly in my arms and stared directly into my face. It was a look I shall never forget, divided equally between fear and regret. I felt my eyes fill, and my chest contract with pity. He was a man I barely knew, yet one to whom I felt most powerfully tuned by circumstance and natural affection.

Mrs Reilly stood at the head of the corridor, holding open a narrow door. When I passed through, stepping sidelong to avoid striking the doctor's feet against the frame, I found myself in a room overlooking the garden. I had neither the opportunity nor the inclination to see how it was arranged – only to notice, in the light of a candle, burned half-way down, which Mrs Reilly must have lit earlier, that the walls were a dark colour, that there was a faint scent of camphor, and that an assortment of vol-

umes lay on the various tables, etc. The whole of my
attention was absorbed by the doctor's bed, which indeed
almost filled the room. It was an old-fashioned canopied
affair, like a large cot, the side-drapes (stitched with
miniature bunches of violets) neatly drawn back, a high
bank of pillows, and the sheet already turned down. Mrs
Reilly was busy filling a glass with water from the pitcher,
and without needing her further instructions I laid the
doctor upon the bed, straightening his limbs. In a further
gesture of pity, I ran my hand across his brow: it felt fever-
ish to my touch, as I had known it would. What I had not
expected was the texture of his skin, which suggested it
might be unusually thick. As I withdrew my hand he let
the handkerchief sink away from his mouth, and shaped
his lips in a silent 'thank you'. His teeth were stained with
blood.

I stood back, noticing for the first time that strange
sensation of dizziness which overcomes us when we
release a weight. Even though I had considered my load a
trifle, I now thought that I might almost float to the ceiling – and certainly swayed. For a moment, therefore, I
may say that I was not wholly in the room, but rather surveying it from a height, careless of my own existence and
concentrating entirely on the doctor and Mrs Reilly. I saw
her place one hand beneath his head, tilting it forward,
his lips opening a little, and his breath making circles on
the liquid. I saw Mrs Reilly's red hair, shining on the ivory
of her cheek. I saw the doctor's hand rise from the sheet
and (accidentally, as I thought) brush lightly against her
breast. It was a soundless scene, yet somehow complete,

like a painting, so that when I returned to myself I was bound to consider my presence a violation. At the same time, I felt compelled to ask what further assistance I might give.

Mrs Reilly told me: none, beyond fetching the new doctor, Mr Garrett, whom Dr Cake had already mentioned, from his house in the village. This I willingly agreed to do, adding that I would not return with him myself, but sheer off to London the following morning, and thence to my home, where I would hope to have good news of Dr Cake's recovery. All this was quickly agreed, after which it only remained for me to make my farewells.

In the circumstances, it was imperative that I did this as speedily as possible – otherwise I should have expressed myself with greater warmth. I merely stood at the doctor's bedside and wished him immediate and better health. To my surprise, for really I did not suppose he had sufficient strength, he lifted his hand and let it lie in my own for a moment, like a sliver of ice.

'Visit us again,' he said, the words coming from his throat in bubbles. 'We have not finished our conversation.' He swallowed, which allowed him to speak more clearly. 'I regret that I have spoken so much of myself. I meant to ask you more. Your work and your writings.'

'They are nothing,' I replied, colouring at this further evidence of his kindness.

'That is not my opinion. Visit us again.' He exerted the faintest pressure on my hand, so that I felt the bones inside his skin, then released it and closed his eyes.

'I shall,' I said, more to Mrs Reilly than the doctor, since he could not make any acknowledgement, then added some expression of my gratitude to her. My last memory is of her breaking into a most beautiful and frank smile, as though a part of her earlier decision had been truly to count me a friend. Whereupon I stepped back from the bed, and made my way rapidly downstairs and out into the evening.

It was not difficult to find the house to which I had been directed, nor to persuade Dr Garrett (an eager young man, who received me dabbing his lips with a napkin) to set off immediately towards his patient. Once the hustle of this activity was over, I returned to the inn for a steak, and gained the privacy of the room in which I am now writing. Such thoughts as occurred to me during my meal are included in my reminiscence of the afternoon, and I shall say no more tonight. Save that it has been a day in which I have seen the pleasure of life, and the pain of death, with unusual clarity. If the doctor is spared, I mean to do everything in my power to accept the honour of his invitation to return.

THREE

The second of Tabor's long recollections of Cake is written, like the first, in nondescript black ink on sheets of ordinary creamy paper. But where the script in the earlier piece is uniform and controlled, here it is careless – many passages are dashed down hastily, and there are several spelling mistakes (which I have silently corrected). In other words, the document is a first draft, and since no second draft survives, this suggests that by the time Tabor started writing it, he had abandoned his plans to publish. The piece was obviously begun, and finished, in the days immediately before Cake's death.

I should not have been surprised to hear nothing more of Dr Cake. On the morning after my first visit to his house, which had ended so abruptly and alarmingly in proof of his illness, I did not attempt to discover news of him (believing that I had already outstayed my welcome), but returned straight to Finchley. Unfortunately my absence had provoked a degree of anxiety in my patients, who punished me for my neglect by demanding my attentions with even more zeal than was customary – so that it was in truth a trial as well as a satisfaction to be among them again. A full week passed before I had sufficient leisure to examine the record of my visit – which, as I had expected, yielded very little that was likely to be of use to my *Survey*. It left me with a general and loose impression of the doctor's humanity, which I valued but could not precisely estimate.

At the same time as I studied my pages, and with a tardiness for which I chastised myself, I wrote the doctor a letter expressing my gratitude for his trouble, and my sincere wish to hear news of his recovery. But I did not honestly expect a reply to this, since I imagined my words would arrive amidst a thousand other turbulences, which would blow them into obscurity. Within a matter of days, however, I received a communication from Mrs Reilly, written on the doctor's behalf and apparently at his dictation, urging me to return to them at my earliest convenience. It was a courteous letter, yet there was something of a command about it; I should have felt summoned, had I not already been so eager to comply.

I confess that I was a little astonished by the excellence of Mrs Reilly's hand-writing, and supposed that she had received instruction from the doctor himself, which I took as a further proof of the intimacy between them. But my consideration of this point was as nothing, compared to the amazement I felt at the request itself. I could only believe that the doctor felt his time on this earth was not long, and that he had professional opinions he would have been sorry not to see included in my *Survey*. I myself now doubted his usefulness on this score, yet my feelings were outweighed by others persuading me I must speak with him. In the time since my return to Finchley, and notwithstanding the burdens upon me, my fascination with the doctor had remained undimmed – and even grown. There were aspects to his life which had impressed me deeply, and matters unconnected with medicine upon which I wished to engage him. I therefore immediately wrote for reassurance that his health could withstand the battering of my questions, was advised (again by Mrs Reilly) that it would, and made plans for my return. Because I expected the pattern of my visit to be the same as before, I advised such patients as I could predict would notice my absence, and set out for Woodham.

It is remarkable, in so short a season as the English Summer, how much change occurs in the look of a land-scape. On my previous journey from Witham, the slow pace of the carriage had allowed me to see the country in its first bloom – the hedgerows thriving with a brilliant electrical greenness, the leaves of beeches still pale from the shelter of their leather buds, the flowers of Spring still lingering at the wayside. Now, in the still heat of an early August afternoon, dust which had been stirred from our road hung over the whole scene, giving it an almost misty appearance. The corn, even more richly spotted with the bright heads of poppies, had burned to a hard gold, and each slope seemed to breathe the warmth of a recumbent human body. It was a display of abundance – of fullness and ripeness – but also of exhaustion, such as our poets have described, and one in particular. The names of villages, where they appeared at all, were frequently obscured by thick clouds of nettle and bramble. At one point my driver came to a complete stop in order to allow the safe passage of a young family of partridges, which insolently bobbed across from one thicket to another. So strong was my impression of generation, and so intense my sense of profusion, that as we reached the little bridge into Woodham, and began to climb the gradient (leaving the Blackwater hidden beneath a skin of lily-pads), I felt I was entering the tunnel which would lead me to another world. I saw everything in a new and more densely shadowed perspective. In this respect, it restored me to the mood of my first visit, in which I had seen Dr Cake, and everything in his house, as though it were not simply shown to me, but somehow etched on my mind, with a peculiar stark clarity.

I paid my driver, resumed my old room in the inn (smaller than I remembered and smelling rankly in the heat), and, after refreshing myself, set off on foot towards the doctor. It was now evening, and the weather of the day had deteriorated. Battalions of charcoal cloud – though fringed with crimson – darkened the Western sky, accompanied by a warm breeze which agitated the trees into a continual low rustling. The effect was to accelerate the passage of the hour, so that as the last cottages fell behind me I seemed to be sinking into the arms of night itself. A fox cub jumped from a low bank into the lane and, finding itself not alone, stared at me boldly before trotting off. A few birds – sparrows and suchlike – jostled on their roosts. A jay landed in a dead elm tree to my right, screeched (too late) its warning of my approach, then swerved away into invisibility: the flash of blue on its wings was as vivid as a kingfisher.

Otherwise the scene was deserted and, with the rising moon making sudden sallies into gaps between the clouds, and the wind deepening its murmur, seemed somewhat threatening. I believe that someone of a more nervous disposition than myself would have taken it as a sign, or warning, or at least returned to the inn for a lantern. As it was, I continued on my way with all the appearance of calm.

It was a pretence I found increasingly difficult to maintain. Not only was I filled with eagerness at the thought of seeing the doctor again, and with anxiety as to his condition, but in the sudden uncertainty of the moment I confess the thought occurred to me that I had missed my way. No friendly house-lights shone ahead of me. No familiar objects appeared in the landscape I passed. Perhaps, I said to myself, scanning the universal blankness, my previous visit to the house had been a kind of fantasy, and the doctor himself a will-o'-the-wisp. It was a preposterous notion, but a proof all the same of how rapidly we may pass from one state of mind to another, and doubt everything we have recently believed or vice-versa. Furthermore, it reminds us how easily we can lose all connection with the ties that bind us to our habitual lives. Standing on that track, with the village invisible behind me, and only the darkness ahead, I supposed that I was alone in the world, with no destination except silence and emptiness. It was a dismaying thought, and reminded me of my insignificance in the scheme of things.

When the clouds melted again – passing overhead without spilling so much as a single drop of rain – I could not believe the darkness had been so intense as I had imagined, and chided myself for entertaining an irresponsible fancy. Yet I proceeded on my way in a more sombre state of mind, which was as well in view of what followed. I reached the edge of the plantation skirting the doctor's property, and followed its line until I arrived at the entrance into his short drive. The gate was shut, and as I manipulated its iron handle, there was a squeal of metal on wood which I thought must have been loud enough to inform Mrs Reilly of my arrival. But there was no movement from the house. Under empty skies, which now contained the true and softer colours of the evening, its white façade was blank as a skull – no sign of life but a feather of smoke emerging from the chimney.

I proceeded to the front step and lifted my hand to knock – whereupon I felt another and unpremeditated change working through me. Strongly as I was drawn to the doctor, and eager as I had been to hear more of his story, I also retained a different kind of curiosity. My hand fell to my side, I stepped away from the door, and made my way silently round the side of the house towards the garden, where my footsteps were entirely soundless. I scarcely knew what I intended, beyond some unacceptable insult to the kindness I had previously received. I can only suppose it was a desire for some new point of view, for some understanding that might derive from my examining the doctor from a distance, rather than more closely, where I felt my personality was a prey to the force of his own more powerful self.

The French windows of his study were closed, but their curtains drawn back to expose the room like a small theatre. Still soundlessly, and more like a criminal than a friend, I smuggled myself into the myrtle bush which knocked its tendrils on the glass, and gazed in. The first object to catch my attention almost caused me to cry aloud and thereby reveal my presence, it surprised me so much. The doctor's bowl of goldfish, lit from behind by two or three large candles, resembled nothing so much as a gigantic eye, confronting my own with the fish passing across in slow circles. Fortunately no sound escaped my lips, and I repositioned myself to look more easily into the room. The doctor, as I had supposed he would be, was lying on his chaise in his customary pose of fretful exhaustion; one half of his face had a horrid pallor, the other was ruddy from the warmth of the fire. His shirt was undone at the collar, his blanket rucked messily round his waist, and with one hand he was pointing at the grate. By depressing a branch of myrtle, I could see Mrs Reilly was kneeling beside the fender, feeding a succession of papers, envelopes, etc, into the flames; it was these that the doctor was urging towards destruction.

No words passed between them, but occasionally Mrs Reilly would turn and look at him. (She had removed her white cap, and the blaze of her red hair was like an echo of the fire itself.) There was reluctance in her movements, which were slow and pensive, and sometimes she would hold up a single sheet of paper, whereupon the doctor nodded as fiercely as he was able, and the item would be burned. When the heap of materials spread round her was exhausted, she rose and crossed the room to the bookcase, withdrew another handful from the drawers which were fitted beneath it, and resumed her place at the hearth. It was a wretched performance, for all the quietness with which it was carried out. Although I did not then guess its whole significance, I was in no doubt that the doctor was overseeing the enactment of a desperate and long-deferred wish: the final ordering of his life before it ended.

Occasionally as I continued to watch this scene, creatures such as spiders and ladybirds would detach themselves from the leaves round about me, and scramble over my face or into my ears. I disliked this extremely, but could do no more than quietly brush them away without disclosing my presence – and gradually became accustomed to their ticklish invasions. So accustomed, in fact, that I do not know how long I might have remained in my seclusion, mesmerised by the dumb-show, had it not been for the doctor himself. On the occasion of Mrs Reilly offering him, yet again, a sheet of writing for his judgement, the nodding of his head was followed by a fit of coughing – not so violent as the last I had seen, but bad enough for Mrs Reilly to abandon her work and perform the even more melancholy task of wiping his brow, holding him by the hand for a few minutes, and after that helping him from his chaise and out of the room – to bed, as I supposed. All these actions were undertaken with the utmost gentleness, so that anyone observing them would have supposed them to be man and wife. The doctor's head lay on her shoulder as they disappeared into the darkness of the hall; her right arm was hooked across his back and pressed against his side.

This, I knew, was a moment at which I could safely leave my place of concealment. But for reasons I did not care to examine closely, I remained where I was, absorbing the look of the room without fear of discovery. With the exception of the papers still strewn across the floor, the open drawers containing yet more stuff, and the fire now sinking in the grate, everything was as I remembered. The volumes on their shelves gave a familiar dull shine; the assorted pictures on the walls, and the cuttings pasted on the screen, continued to offer their frozen dramas of bravery or love; the linnet clung in silence to the rail in its cage, so still this evening I supposed she must have been asleep. But it was not so much the things in themselves which held my attention. It was the suggestion they made of a whole life – their plain demonstration of how each of us describes our existence by means of objects which are indifferent to us, which survive us, and which are then thrown back into the common stock from which they are soon gathered again and ascribed other roles in new circumstances. The room, that is to say, was a tableau of what is arresting in the human pageant – and its pathos was made all the greater by the peculiarity of my vantage point. During the confusion I had suffered on my journey to the house, I had felt the usual boundaries of experience loosen. Now, with my face pressed to the glass of the doctor's window, I felt that I had slipped outside life entirely, and could survey its conditions and limits. The experience was demoralising and quickening in equal parts.

I soon turned from these speculations to a more humdrum question: namely, should I emerge from my hiding place and return directly to the inn, or make my presence known to Mrs Reilly? The latter course seemed the more courteous, always provided she had finished attending to the doctor – and in order to allow time for her to do this, I resolved to remain hidden for a moment longer. The decision now appears strange to me since, as I say, it was intended as a courtesy, yet involved me in further deception. At the time I did not perceive a contradiction. I was too thoroughly engrossed to judge anything with a proper degree of clarity.

Emerging from the shadows with as little noise and as much dignity as possible, and at last wiping my face and neck thoroughly clean of insects, etc, I found myself meandering further into the garden, following the glimmering line of the flower-border, observing the enormous mass of the laurel bower, and eventually coming to the glass-house. I walked like someone in a trance, the cool, moist twilight rippling over my face, my feet scarcely seeming to touch the ground. The effect was to redouble the sensation which had previously affected me in the lane. But for a reason I had no curiosity to explain, it no longer generated a feeling of solitude, rather of integration and belonging, as though I had become a part of the silent kingdom around me – the universe of drooping leaves and soaked grass-blades, of sleeping birds and blundering moths.

The glass-house door stood ajar, and I squeezed through without altering its position and stepped onto the brick floor. The air immediately wrapped itself round me in a warm bandage. It was not simply the fact that it had stewed all the long summer's day which made it so palpable; it was the added burden of flower-scent which weighed me down. The doctor's orchids, clearly visible in spite of the darkness of the hour, seemed to turn enquiringly towards me. Some were shaped like the open mouths of snakes, exposing the pale interior of their throats; others were like miniature bells; others again resembled caps or bonnets – and all were the colour of fantasy, not of life. Deep royal purples. Pulsing yellow, spotted with blood-flecks. Crimson blushing into magenta. When I had first glimpsed them across the garden a few weeks before, they had seemed exotic and delightful. Now they were obviously repellent. Rearing on spindly stalks, shockingly bare of surrounding leaves (though with some flopping from the mossy earth around each base), they seemed to hiss, or gasp, or pant, or in some other way to strain upon the atmosphere, as if to appear breathless were their natural condition.

Faced with such a phantasmagoria, the dullest mind would soon shift its thinking from the flowers themselves to their owner and curator. I did so immediately. I imagined the doctor in the candle-lit cavern of his bed, his shining head propped on the pillow, perhaps at this moment accepting a glass offered by Mrs Reilly. He would not live to see the flowers he had nurtured shrivel on their stalks and fall; I understood that. What I did not know – what no man can ever truly know about another – was the exact mood of his reflections on the subject. In my own work as a doctor I have seen hundreds die – men, women and children – and have been astonished by the diversity of their response. Wizened old stoics have become blubbering infants. Infants have become stoics. Devout virgins have turned clamorous for the life they denied when it was full of opportunity. Sinners have shown a greater understanding of virtue than clerics who made it their whole study. I have been able to draw only one conclusion from my observations: that our greatest human talent is our gift for ignoring death while we are still secure in our possession of life, and that as soon as our hold is weakened, and we know it must soon be broken, we discover aspects of ourselves that we previously did not know existed. In this respect our deaths may be considered our greatest moment of revelation, and produce a self-knowledge which it is our tragedy never to enjoy. Truly, the greatest secret we take to our graves is the understanding of ourselves.

I discovered with some degree of disgust that the heat of the glass-house had made me break into a sweat. My shirt was clinging to my back, and my whole face moist. But whether I had endured the warmth for a moment or for several minutes I could not say, being lost in the labyrinth of my reflections. When I stepped out into the garden again I drew a handkerchief from my pocket and patted myself dry – conscious, for the second time, that anyone looking on would reckon me a comical if not a disreputable figure. On this occasion, the thought was enough to recall me to what I considered my usual character, and it was therefore with some embarrassment, and no little shame, that I retraced the route of my trespass, and brought myself at last to the front door of the house. As I arrived, I heard one or two pigeons stirring in the dark trees either side of the drive, clapping their wings sleepily, then settling again.

A single knock brought Mrs Reilly to the threshold carrying a candle. With her free hand she was twisting her hair beneath her bonnet, which I knew she must only that moment have put on. I apologised for the lateness of my visit, and pretended that I had recently arrived in the village, but she did not appear in the least surprised to see me. In fact by comparison with the severity she had shown on my previous visit, her manner suggested that she now considered me an old and trusted friend. She explained that the doctor's health had declined since I had seen him last, and that this very evening he had suffered a bad fit of coughing – always speaking in a low whisper which her accent made difficult to understand. Since I already knew what she was telling me, this hardly mattered.

'Shall I come up to him?' I asked, meaning in a professional capacity.

Mrs Reilly assured me that this would not be necessary, as I had anticipated she would, but invited me to return in the morning after breakfast, when she was confident the doctor would be pleased to see me.

I told her that I happily accepted her invitation, then after a pause added 'Mrs Reilly' in a curious level voice I hardly recognised as my own. I was uncertain of what I wanted to tell her, or to hear, only that I should not let this moment pass without some further contact between us.

'Yes?' she asked in a tentative voice which nevertheless was loud enough to disturb the pigeons again in the trees behind me, and set them fussing on their roosts.

'It is nothing,' I said. 'It will keep for tomorrow. Good night.'

I looked across the thin flame of her candle to her face at once suffused and hollowed in its glow, expecting her merely to repeat my own last word. But to my surprise and pleasure she was more forthcoming.

'It was not always like this,' she said simply.

'You mean . . .?'

'The doctor was not always like this.'

'Of course not,' I said, with an embarrassed laugh. Mrs Reilly seemed to be telling me something so obvious, it hinted awkwardly at other reasons why she might be detaining me.

Then she laughed herself – a low gliding sound. 'No, indeed, of course not. I should have been more direct, and said I wish that you had seen him when he was well.'

'He was obviously a remarkable man,' I said, realising (and not for the first time) how dull my own remarks seemed when compared to Mrs Reilly's or the doctor's.

'Remarkable is the least of it,' she came back at me, more quickly now. 'He was more vigorous than a man half his age. More . . .' She moved her candle in a small circle, so its light flared and shrank and blossomed again across her face. 'More wonderful. More passionate,' she went on. 'Everyone loved him for it. You can understand why – I can tell that. But you can never understand it in a feeling way, since you have only seen him suffering. And now you will always think of him as someone dying, whereas I shall think of his dying as an aberration. For me he will always be someone in health. In his prime.'

As Mrs Reilly spoke the last three words her voice shook and her head dropped. I took the opportunity to look at her more directly. Little mis-shapes of redness had come into her cheeks and were soaking down onto the white skin of her throat, so that for a moment she seemed less like the capable woman I knew her to be, and respect-ed, than a girl I might care for with a different sort of ten-derness. But I stood still, doing no more than let her words drop into my imagination. They had the effect of deepening my sadness at every sign of the weakness I had seen in the doctor, by drawing my attention to the oppo-site. In my mind's eye I saw him striding through the vil-lage and surrounding lanes, knocking eagerly on doors, always somehow in the sun. I felt, with an immediate and definite pressure, the force of his goodness.

'I can never know what you have known about him,' I said softly. 'But I can imagine it, I promise you.'

At this Mrs Reilly looked up again and met my eye. She smiled – a slow smile – and extended the candle towards me, so I felt its heat on my face like a kiss, then drew it back once more. But she said nothing.

And I said nothing more myself, knowing that whatever words I spoke would have betrayed stronger emotions than I wanted to show. I merely bowed my own head slowly, and stepped out of the circle of her light, then turned and walked quickly away down the drive. When I reached the gate and looked back again, the door to the house was closed and Mrs Reilly had disappeared. The thought that I had been so gracefully welcomed, and had been made privy to such exquisite feeling, having haunted the place like a common burglar, made me creep up the lane to the inn like a guilty thing. Mrs Reilly, I supposed, would have extinguished her light even before I reached my room. Extinguished her light, having first collected the papers by the hearth, perhaps to revive the fire by feeding them into the embers, perhaps to return them to the drawers in the bookcase, and await the doctor's further instructions.

Four

Tabor's manuscript continued on a separate sheet of the same creamy paper.

The following morning, after a night of more distur-bances than dreams (thanks to the exertions of the church clock), I rose in time to dissuade the inn-keeper from providing me with a bacon breakfast I had not ordered, and to request a simpler affair of egg and bread. I suppose it was excitement which quenched my appetite. All my interest was directed towards my meeting with the doctor, which I knew would certainly be my last. As soon as my meal was done, I set out towards his house.

On a little-known road, memory plays strange tricks. The things we believed were close together seem far apart, and objects we remembered as enormous are in fact small. So it was for me on my short journey. The precise spot by a clump of decayed cow-parsley, where I had stood only a few hours before and watched the charcoal clouds roll towards me, had seemed at the time a substan-tial distance from the village. Now it appeared but a step away – and, moreover, was bathed in a mild and steady sunlight which carried no hint of the turbulence it had recently witnessed. Everywhere I looked – at the bowed grasses by the roadside, at the briony and other hedge flowers, at the clumps of shining blackberries – there was nothing but evidence of peace and plenty. This impression was made all the stronger by a breeze which, as it swayed the fields of corn in a regular wave-pattern, made the entire landscape heave like the sea. It was a striking proof, if proof were needed, that the truth of what we observe lies less in things themselves, than in the mood of the observer.

Fortified by this evidence of the power we humans have over our circumstances, I reached the doctor's door in a matter of moments. Here too there was no sign of the commotion of the previous evening – no smoke from the chimney, no dew upon the ground to show my foot prints winding into the garden. Nothing but calm early sunlight on the house – and Mrs Reilly opening the door while the echo of my knock still resounded through the hall. Her appearance confirmed the impression of serenity. With her cap freshly washed (and her pretty face too, judging by its glow), she gave me a shy smile, then showed me towards the doctor's study. This smile was the only sign that anything might have recently passed between us.

While we were entering the gloom of the hall, Mrs Reilly whispered that her master was 'better this morning', but in such a pensive way that this 'better' did not mean all it might have done. I laid my hat upon the table, and nodded towards her gratefully, feeling that this was not the moment for a longer conversation. I was eager to see the doctor, and had no wish to complicate my feelings for him with reflections of a different sort.

Considering that I am writing this account several days after the events described, and am therefore likely (despite my best efforts) to have forgotten the exact sequence and phrasing of what occurred, I hope that I may be granted some licence in attempting its reconstruction. I have invented nothing, only added a necessary fluency here and there, so as to make the time seem both leisurely and urgent – which indeed it was.

The doctor's room was exactly as I had remembered it: the same dim hush emanating from the prints and books, the same profusion of light from the French window, the same soft density and warmth. Taking it all in with a sigh of appreciation, I advanced immediately beyond the protection of the screen, and found the doctor lying before me on his chaise, dressed in clean linen like Mrs Reilly. I stopped still for a moment to regard him. His face (which I had not seen clearly the previous night) struck me as being noticeably more haggard – the lips still full and vivid, but the skin around the mouth tightened, so that it was dragged permanently open. His breath, too, betrayed his condition, sounding in a series of painfully drawn and distinct gasps, with an occasional horrible gurgling undertow that threatened to stifle him.

As soon as he saw me his face brightened, and the sadness I had observed in him was banished. 'Dr Tabor,' he said, indicating the chair at his side. 'Do you come to me as a poet or a physician?'

The question so completely exposed the matter I had

hoped to keep hidden for a while, that I believe I actually blushed. But as I did his bidding, and took my appointed place, he took pity on me and spared me the trouble of an answer. 'It is no matter,' he went on. 'You may come as either or both. You are a healing influence in any case.'

My blush, which should have deepened further at this, receded, and it was only pleasure I felt when leaning forward to press his hand. He let it lie in my own for a moment, regarding the two together. 'I have an old man's hands,' he said. 'It has always been so, even when I was young.' Then he sighed, releasing me and sinking back. The breath from his mouth was so stale, I straightened in spite of myself, glancing round the room. Everything was as it had been: the linnet, the pictures, the goldfish, the paraphernalia of tablets, little tinctured bottles and books at his elbow. In the fireplace, the grate had been swept clean, then laid with new sheets of crumpled newspaper, on which were arranged strips of kindling, and a spray of rosemary. The scent of ash, mingled with sweetness, overlay the smell of decay that came from the doctor.

'Polly still seems contented with the world,' I said, with a futile kind of courtesy, indicating the bird in her cage. (In truth the creature did not look in the best of spirits, being huddled into a dingy green bundle on her perch.)

'Oh, Polly is always a good influence,' replied the doctor with a smile. 'Whatever our own condition might actually be, we always imagine her well and happy, and so benefit ourselves.'

I nodded, uncertain how to continue, but the doctor put me at my ease by changing direction.

'We must not be so wayward in our conversation as before,' he told me, speaking comfortably now and closing his eyelids while he spoke. 'I shall not be content if you leave me today with a feeling that I have given you no help in your work.'

'That is not the only reason I am here,' I answered, without a shadow of my original uncertainty.

'I understand that.' The doctor opened one eye, which gave him the look of a mischief-maker, then closed it again. 'I understand that, and we shall come to your other reasons in due course. But tell me first, what impressions do you have of our village, its conditions and so forth?'

The simplicity of this question allowed me to see how our talk might develop, and I replied with as much consideration as I could muster, telling him that the cottages around the main street seemed comfortable and well-maintained, and the health of the people good. My intention was in part to compliment him on the lifetime of care he had bestowed; also to suggest that I had seen worse suffering elsewhere.

'The best I can say of my life,' he said when I had finished, 'is that I have worked at a time when the cure for sickness seemed a possible thing. And the thought of this has borne me up. For there are parts of my practice which are not so reassuring as those you have seen. Places of dreadful deprivation and wretchedness.' Here he paused for a moment and swallowed carefully. 'Yet we cannot entirely blame injustice for their existence. They are an inevitable part of our humanity. They –'

I cleared my throat to interrupt, fearing that such a

long series of opinions would provoke another fit of coughing. But the doctor was on a course he had prepared, and would not be deflected. Holding one hand in the air like an orator subduing a crowd, he continued.

'I will say it again. I have seen entire families hereabouts, living in the most miserable poverty – cellars, without the slightest drainage, with every drop of wet and every scrap of dirt having to be carried up into the street. Dens where a free man would think it a crime for any creature to live, but where a rent is demanded and cannot be found if work or health fails. I have seen all this, and scarcely felt able to speak of "houses" or "employment". If you need evidence for your studies, I shall give you instructions so that you may see for yourself.'

In the heat of his condemnation, the doctor had lost the original direction of his thought, but I did not correct him immediately. Instead, I described to him a number of cases from my own experience at Finchley, in which families of eight or nine children were squeezed into places so small, and so disgusting, sickness has been inevitable. While I did this the doctor gave signs of assent, the phlegm whispering in his throat. 'We may see in this,' he said at length, 'evidence of the Act. The improvements were welcome – profoundly welcome – but they have left us with an infinity of need.'

'And when you spoke of the inevitable results of our humanity?' I said, guiding him back towards his path.

'It is an immense question,' he replied. 'I meant that we should imagine a world in which all burdens have been lifted, all inequalities resolved, all injustices addressed –

and ask ourselves how mankind would then behave. Do you suppose a mood of universal kindness would prevail? I think not. We have seen too much evil and jealousy in men who have no cause to harbour such feelings. We know that we should be forever devising new ways of imposing burdens in the name of bettering ourselves. This is what I mean about inevitable results. I mean that the inequalities we perceive, and the wretchedness, are not only the particular consequence of a system that obtains at present, but of a fault in ourselves that can never be destroyed. I have, I know, a certain morbidity in my temperament, and a willingness to brood on evil, but this is my considered opinion nevertheless.'

As the doctor came to the end of this rhodomontade (I shall use his own word again), a single cough caused him to shudder, and I took the liberty of using my handkerchief to wipe his brow. This required me to lean forward so that my face was close to his own. I had expected to catch the scent of his sickness, as before, but Mrs Reilly had done her work well: it was not the staleness of sweat I inhaled, but a delicate lemony fragrance, which seemed to emanate from all his clothes.

'I did not always think so,' the doctor continued, keeping his eyes straight ahead as if he did not choose to notice my ministrations, and speaking very quietly. 'In my youth I had a greater trust in humanity, and believed that to discover its nobility only required an adequate amount of freedom. Freedom, combined with a good genius, and the willingness to attempt a voyage of the intellect. Experience has taught me otherwise, and has given a Quakerish cast to my reflections. I have learned to consider uneasiness a habitual sensation.'

'But you have given yourself to others!' I expostulated. It is generally embarrassing to pay compliments to a person, but in this case I did not find it so. The doctor had done himself an injustice (and I dare say that I considered my own professional efforts to have been slighted in the process).

'Ah,' said the doctor, wandering somewhere between a word and a mere noise. 'I have given myself to others, that is true. I have felt the glory of patriotism, and of making a country happier. But as I have done so I have also lost the fine point of my spirit.'

'In what sense?'

'Idealism. Hopefulness.' He delivered the words as if he were laying down stones at my feet, and then added a third. 'Ambition.'

I hesitated, confused that he should say such things, having so recently painted a rosy picture of the future of our profession. In truth, I should not have been so baffled. The doctor was doing no more than describe a difference between his own condition and the situation in general. Nevertheless, I did not immediately seize this point, simple as it now appears, and in the hope that my delay would seem like a natural reflection, followed the doctor's example in gazing beyond the window. A small flock of sheep – unnoticed on my previous visits to the house – were munching busily among the docks and buttercups. With a part of my mind I knew that it would be reasonable for me to refute the doctor's last remarks, and to say that he had in fact fulfilled his ambition by working so diligently for his patients. With another part of myself I wanted to accept it. I knew it was the means by which I could change the subject of our conversation into something I more sincerely wanted to address.

When I turned back to face him, he was regarding me with a clarity which dissolved all my doubts. The effect was to discourage further conversation, and instead to lure me into a dream. It was not one I expected to have at this particular moment, since I still regarded it as a kind of presumption, and would have preferred to postpone it until later in our meeting, or after it had ended. But since it came when it did, and I am bound to be truthful in my recollections of the doctor, I shall describe it now. In the silence of that long moment I saw – as if from nowhere – a ship ploughing through rough seas, with dolphins gambolling through the waves alongside, and phosphor shining. I saw a young man hovering between life and death in the darkness of a cabin, and another young man, his friend, attending him. The same ship then swerved into the choppier waters of the Mediterranean, and thence to a wide harbour. Now the two friends jolted on an open road, passing through marshland and occasional meagre villages, until they reached their destination, which was a door beside a fountain, a narrow room, and a ceiling with painted flower-heads.

There followed the ghastly drama of a sick-bed – the young man wasting on a sweat-soaked sheet, crying out sometimes in pain and rage, while his friend brought him little meals of rice. I heard the fountain battering in its basin, the tramp and murmur of indifferent crowds going about their business in the world. I watched sunlight fade from the window in the evening, then return after an interval. Indeed, it is beyond the power of my pen to describe properly the agony of that room. In my vision, I felt the sickness of the young man as if it were my own: the humiliation of his poverty and dependency, the pointless and unjustified fury with himself for having been made to fail (as he thought) in his ambitions, the utter desolation of his removal from all but one of his friends – and from the one who loved him best. In the history of human suffering, it stands apart: most bitter, pathetic and undeserved. A tragedy of tragedies – yet, as I say, all concentrated at that moment into a single compact picture.

Compact, but I confess not entirely self-contained. For the instant in which I saw everything I have described, also revealed the inevitable end towards which it all tended. The extinction of life. A dead man on the sick-bed. An incalculable and irreparable loss.

Yet that is not what appeared to me. In place of the sick-bed I observed the passing of a crisis – the young man (for whom all hope had been abandoned) gradually recovering his strength, the colour returning to his cheek, his arm stronger as he accepted a plate of food, the shutters of the window pushed wide to receive the warmth of the Spring, the sun slanting across the floor, the young man relishing the miracle of his vigour.

The miracle. I was vouchsafed a glimpse of it which cannot have lasted more than a single second, yet even something so brief was enough to make me feel astonished at my boldness in imagining such a thing. It was an event which all available evidence made impossible. Truly, it was an absurdity – or would have been (I told myself, with a degree of calm calculation which surprised me) were it not for the doctor's insinuations, and my own willingness to believe them.

This was the conundrum I faced, which I had not previously dared to present so candidly to myself. Was I to believe facts as I had been told them – facts that all the world accepted? Or was I to believe the evidence as it appeared to be unfolding before me. Supposing that I might have fallen under the spell of a delusion, I asked myself who was responsible. The doctor, who had led me to my conclusion with lies and flatteries? Or myself? It was a question I could not immediately solve; it was too momentous.

All the while I had been dreaming, the doctor had not altered his expression, but merely regarded me with a steady coolness. Now he brought me back to myself as gently as if he were waking a sleeping child. 'You do not interrogate that word,' he said quietly. 'That word ambition.'

I looked at him without speaking for a moment, while the dregs of everything I had just seen and thought began to settle on the floor of my mind. Eventually I was ready with my answer. 'I understand,' I said in the same level tone as his own. And then again: 'I understand.'

There was no reply, but a glance across my shoulder into the banked kindling of the fire, then at the portrait of our Presider on the wall above. So responsive did I now feel to the doctor's presence (or so misled was I) that I interpreted this look as containing both admonishment and encouragement. I advised myself that he would not accept a direct approach to our subject; it must only be circled and seen sideways. Like a shy bird in a thicket, which will take flight at the least disturbance.

'You were good enough . . . ,' I began, straightening in my chair and speaking with a nervous formality as I considered how best to continue. 'You were good enough to ask me about my verses, the last time we met. I told you I considered them as belonging to a different part of my existence, and I spoke the truth. Yet the deepest desires of our youth never leave us entirely, however we might find a different expression for them. Do you agree?'

My voice sounded somewhat loud, after the quietness of our recent exchange, but the doctor was not disturbed by this. He seized on my question bravely and answered it at length – speaking, once again, as though he were repeating a speech he had rehearsed for me.

'I have led a useful life, and I am not too creeping to deny it. I have put it to the service of others, which was what I intended. Yet it can hardly be described as a remarkable one, and in that respect I have dashed the hopes of my youth, which were to prove myself exceptional. Yet who is to say whether it is more valuable to be exceptional than useful? And who is to say whether the achievements of our youth will have the same effect if we repeat them in age? It may be that we are destined to live different lives within our single span, and that to continue in one course and one course alone is an offence to nature. Think of the great writers. None but Shakespeare' – his eyes danced to the portrait behind me – 'none but he has proved the value of a single application throughout his whole existence. You will say Milton, but even he has some falling off. Wordsworth is an example of the type I mean.'

He stared at me, no doubt anticipating the reply I gave in due course. 'You know how I have revered Wordsworth. We have spoken of him already.'

'We have. But it is the young Wordsworth to whom you give your allegiance, and not the veteran who now preaches at us. Am I right? Supposing Wordsworth had ceased upon the midnight some thirty years since. What would we have lost? Might he not have been better advised to give all his energies to the Post Office, and improve that operation, rather than trouble us with his homilies?'

'But . . .'

'No.' The doctor lifted his hand again, in his old manner of dismissal. 'Wordsworth's anxiety for humanity has faded, or his means to express that anxiety. There is no difference as far as his readers are concerned.'

'But,' I persevered, determined not to be deflected from my way by the doctor's practised answers, 'might it not be the case that by continuing to test himself, to explore within, he might eventually discover again the passions of his youth?'

The doctor frowned, not unkindly, but with a pout of disappointment. 'Impossible. And I am surprised to hear you put the question, since your own practice suggests you do not believe it yourself.'

'I can only repeat what I said at our first meeting,' I said, a little offended. 'I am not Wordsworth. When I examine the achievements of my youth they are nothing, or next to nothing. I do not have his achievements to remember or to emulate. I have no backwards longings.'

'Time will decide your achievements, Dr Tabor,' said the doctor wearily, as though I had forgotten a commonplace. 'We have already agreed on that.' Then he rallied again and spoke more briskly. 'And I shall press my point by asking you to consider Coleridge. He was one whose poetical powers lasted for a shorter time than Wordsworth's, but who saved himself by adaptation.'

'You mean by lectures and suchlike.'

'I mean giving us disquisitions on the art, rather than the art itself. I would ask you again: if such a change were out of the question, might it not be better to abandon the attempt entirely?' Here he swallowed, and dropped his voice a little. 'Might it not even be better to die than to continue?'

'You are thinking of Shelley.'

The doctor nodded. 'I am thinking of Shelley, of Burns, of poor John Clare. Might it not be the case that we think of them as well as we do because, in being denied life, they were also denied the opportunity to disappoint us?'

Two spots of red had appeared in the doctor's cheeks as he spoke. I was shocked by his question, but saw that I must not lose my chance to match it. I was now closer than ever before to the point of intimacy I wished to gain.

'You have not mentioned Keats,' I said, unsure whether I expected the doctor to shoulder aside my words with an easy remark, or to engage with them directly. In the event, the reaction was unlike anything I had predicted. I heard (heard not saw, since it was concealed on the further side of the screen) the door to the study whisk open and Mrs Reilly advance so quickly into view that her footsteps shook the ornaments which were placed around the room. I had forgotten what I had noticed before, namely her habit of listening in secret to my conversations with the doctor, and now found her regarding us in the manner of a judge. Her arms were folded across her bosom, her lips were pressed tight, her face was white as paper (though still spotted with freckles), and she rocked silently from heel to toe.

'Mrs Reilly,' said the doctor, with no element of surprise in his voice. 'Dr Tabor and I were discussing the various means of making and preserving a reputation. We had come to the interesting case of John Keats.'

Mrs Reilly gave a little nod, though whether to express acceptance or exasperation, I could not tell. I regarded her steadily. Hitherto, her various interruptions of our conversation had been decisive. Assuming the relative modesties of her position, she had nevertheless seemed to have the last word on every proceeding – as secretary, as nurse, as a figure of conscience. Now, as I say, she seemed on the point of resigning her authority and collaborating with the doctor in his own independent decision. I found myself smiling at her, in the way that a child smiles at a parent when he expects to be punished, and for a full minute she did nothing. Then her mouth relaxed, her arms uncrossed, she fetched a low chair from the further part of the room, and she sat down beside me. I caught the wholesome smell of lemon and starch as she settled herself – the same that I had recently noticed on the doctor.

'It will not disturb you if I join you?' she said, matter-of-fact. 'In case I am required.'

'By no means,' I said, too quickly, feeling that I had spoken out of turn. But the doctor made no objection. He stretched one hand across his rug and towards Mrs Reilly, which she affected not to see. 'Dr Tabor is right,' he said. 'We would be grateful for your opinion when you have one.'

'Oh, I shall have no opinion,' she replied. 'Only an interest.'

'As you wish,' said the doctor, folding his hands on his stomach once more. He blinked his eyes, gathering himself, then glanced at the linnet (still bunched in silence) before fixing his attention upon the goldfish in their bowl. Their idle circlings took them from being their own shapes and sizes through the distortions of the glass into becoming strange freaks and monsters, then back to themselves again.

'In the context we have already created,' began the doctor, 'the case of Keats is highly instructive. Let us remind ourselves. Keats departed this world some twenty years ago.'

'Twenty-three,' I interrupted, and felt Mrs Reilly inclining her head beside me, in a gesture of what I took to be agreement.

'Very well. Twenty-three. And in a state of neglect, or of actual disparagement, that set him apart.'

'With respect, Dr Cake,' I interjected again, 'your saying "neglect" hardly does justice to the reality.' I was shocked with myself for speaking so boldly on a matter I suspected the doctor to understand very well, but the power of my recent vision was still upon me, and drove me forward. 'Keats's death was in every respect one of the most wretched – though of course you are right to suggest there are some who say he was killed by reviewers.'

The doctor gave no sign of being offended by my outburst, but on hearing its final phrase he uttered a single bark of laughter, loud enough for me to feel concerned that he might yet injure himself. 'So it is said. So Shelley said, in the poem which did him much credit and Keats a little – and credulous minds have agreed. But consider.' He raised one finger to his lips, as if requesting the silence that already surrounded him. 'We have spoken before of reviewers and the hurt they can give – their venom and stupidity. A man would be a fool who said they had no power.' His hand dropped from his face, and he looked eagerly from Mrs Reilly's face to my own. 'And yet no man, however bold in his imaginings, is entirely alone to face their assaults. He has friends and interpreters to console him. To speak for him. Keats had a gift for friendship – he had Hunt, and Reynolds and Woodhouse and all the rest. He had Hazlitt' – here his head rocked slowly from side to side – 'though Hazlitt did not speak as warmly in print as he had in person. These were all people whose opinions were of more value to Keats than the slanders of Lockhart.'

'Tennyson would say the same,' I put in – partly, I admit, to give the doctor a pause and allow him to recover his strength a little. 'I only mean,' I added, 'that Lockhart, who is supposed to have killed Keats, also made an attempt on the life of Tennyson.'

'I do not know Tennyson,' said the doctor, then added in a hurry, 'I have only read him. A very conscious poet, and capable of great beauty. And certainly there was a period in which he paid the price for his loyalty to Keats. But we think he is safe now, do we not? Reviewers could not murder Tennyson, any more than they could murder Keats. The only difference is that Tennyson has lived to reap his harvest.'

Now it was Mrs Reilly's turn to relieve the doctor from his exertions. Sitting completely still in her chair, and speaking with the confidence of one perfectly acquainted with her own opinions, she said, 'If anything killed Mr Keats it was time and illness.'

'Killed him in what sense?' asked the doctor immediately, with nothing in his voice to suggest that he was not speaking to an equal, and debating a topic familiar to both of them. 'As we reminded ourselves before, Keats died with as small a reputation as it is possible for a man to have – yet nowadays what do we find? An Italian edition of his poems. An English edition of the same. Not much I grant you, and very little regarded; but a proof of something. Furthermore' – he pulled at the blanket which lay across him, smoothing and flattening it – 'I have reason to believe that a memoir is in preparation.'

While the doctor said this I leaned back in my chair and examined him with as great a degree of objectivity as I could manage. If my suspicions were well-founded, it was a remark of extraordinary daring. One which risked provoking me into the formulation of numerous further questions, any one of which might be embarrassing to him. Yet even as this realisation flashed upon me, I saw that what might be a sort of teasing insouciance in his manner (the little smile which played about his mouth) could equally well be a sign that he knew I had accepted the rules of our conversation, and would not press him. He was, in other words, not so much careless in this reference to the Memoir, as grateful. Grateful for the fact of its existence, and grateful for my complicity.

'I have heard as much myself,' I said, endeavouring to keep my voice free from anything that might imply superior knowledge. 'I believe that the author has benefited from previous attempts to produce such a thing.'

'Richard Monckton Milnes,' the doctor said with a slow relish, as if he were eating a fruit. 'Lord Houghton. You have obviously seen the advertisements. We live out of the way here, but we have seen them as well, have we not, Mrs Reilly?' Then he frowned, and a shadow seemed to pass across him. 'It may be, of course, that I do not see the volume itself, but I have the interest of knowing it will exist. This is all I meant to prove earlier, when I spoke of reviewing and the rest. Posterity is your only true judge. Posterity and the opinion we have of ourselves.'

'You are right,' I said with a readiness I could not conceal, and a determination to press on with the task I had set myself. 'But let us suppose for a moment that a man were able to view the achievements of his life from the vantage of posterity. What would he then think?'

I felt, but did not dare to see, Mrs Reilly stirring beside me as I spoke, running the open palm of one hand nervously up and down against her dress.

'What would he then think?' repeated the doctor, with a slight widening of his eyes.

'Yes,' I persisted. 'To continue with Keats. How would he have regarded the successes of his youth, supposing he had been able to view them across a distance of time?'

'He did not know they were successes,' replied the doctor quickly.

'That is not what I mean,' I said, with a deliberate doggedness. 'I mean supposing he had lived to see what had first been adjudged failures, or caviar for the few, become favoured by the many – as we are beginning to see they are. You have said that posterity is our only judge, and in this case the truth would surely have been . . .'

'Delightful,' the doctor broke in, as if I had been faltering, which was not the case. 'Keats in his youth dreamed of living in the very mouth of fame, as a reward for believing that he could not live without poetry. To know that these hopes had been realised – why, it would have sent him to his grave a happier man. There is nothing ambiguous about this.'

I understood from the doctor's brisk tone that he disliked the topic and wanted to see it closed. But in a mood of rebellion which surprised even myself, I observed: 'There seems to be some doubt in your voice – though your conclusion, as you say, is not a controversial one.'

'Well,' said the doctor, with a peremptory suddenness I had not noticed in him before. Once again, his hands fluttered over the blanket, smoothing out wrinkles which did not in fact exist. Mrs Reilly, whose own agitation was manifesting itself in a sharper inclination of her head towards the doctor, evidently felt his unhappiness as if it were her own.

'Are you comfortable, doctor?' she asked superfluously.

The effect of her interruption was to rally him. 'Quite comfortable,' he replied, in the same hard voice he had recently used with me. 'I was merely considering how best to answer Doctor Tabor, that is all. The presentation of facts is an easy thing; the imagining of one mind into another is a most mysterious form of semi-speculation.'

'Of course, Sir,' said Mrs Reilly, dropping at once into her deferential style, and re-composing herself in her seat.

The doctor cleared his throat carefully. 'When you say there is doubt in my voice, doctor, you are not exactly right. Doubt is not what I feel on this subject. It is more nearly awe. Consider. A man who had achieved great things, saw them enter the world without reward or recognition, and then died in ignorance of their eventual success: this would be a torment, would it not? But a torment which in terms of the everlasting would only agitate a ghost. Would it not be much worse for the man who lived to see his success, and not claim it as his own?'

'That is what I mean,' I said gently.

'Exactly,' replied the doctor. His face had darkened, as if he were grappling with a headache – and as I perceived it, he had indeed worked himself into the very corner where I wished him to be. Any pleasure or relief I felt upon noticing this, however, was immediately overshadowed by concern at the sight of how painfully he laboured. 'To be tantalised in that way . . . ,' he went on slowly. 'It would be a torment worthy of Purgatory. Whatever the pleasures of seeing a just reward come in at last, they would be quite undermined by the sensation of helplessness. Of knowing that you were time's plaything.' His last words came brokenly, and eventually ceased altogether. I said nothing, but sat still and watched him.

'I cannot give you the plain answer you expect,' he said at length, avoiding my eye. 'Except to say this. For a man who still hankers after his former self, his young self, it would be insufferable to have continual knowledge of the deprivation. But for a man who has made a complete separation with his past it would be acceptable – even a pleasant sort of freedom. All of us who have not died young must suppose that we live a number of separate existences. In this case, we must accept that Keats, had he lived, would not have been any different from the next man. He would have made his accommodations. He would have welcomed his new busy-ness.'

'Suppose?' I said, still quietly, but with a guilty determination not to lose my chance. 'Or hope?'

The doctor stilled his fidgeting and looked at me directly. I saw once again that some redness had come into his cheeks – not the warm red of excitement or health, but the chilly colour of distress. Immediately, I regretted that I had been so obstinate in my enquiries, and knew that I must desist, or risk losing his co-operation altogether. But as I opened my mouth to ask a different and less compromising question, he gave me his answer.

'Hope,' he said. Even though the utterance was brief, almost like a sigh, it gave me the information I needed. I smiled, and nodded my head.

At this Mrs Reilly rose to her feet, wiping the palms of her hands on her skirt, and thereby showing her relief. I understood that for all her appearance of calm, she believed a confrontation had been faced and avoided. When she announced that she would fetch us refreshment from the kitchen, and return with it directly, I took it as a sign that she was sure I would not violate the web of discretions in which we were all enmeshed. I told her that I would be glad of some tea to drink, and kept silent until she had left the room.

Mrs Reilly had good reason to trust me. I had no intention of taking a more direct approach to the doctor, since I understood it would produce a denial, or a show of incomprehension. Yet at the same time I considered that I was becoming an expert at indirection, and was resolved to continue in the same circuitous manner.

'You were saying' (I examined the fingernails of one hand as I spoke, to suggest my remarks were merely trifling) 'that you considered Keats to have been in a sense fortunate to have died when he did.'

'Not fortunate exactly.' Even though Mrs Reilly had been almost entirely silent while sitting with us, the fact of her absence made the doctor appear undefended. His voice now seemed larger than before, more resonant and yet at the same time transparent, as though his words were echoes and not substantial things. 'No man's death can be considered a fortunate thing. And yet it is true that Keats was spared the unhappiness of seeing his gift diminish. In the same way that Shelley was spared, and Wordsworth has not been.'

'But who is to say it would have diminished? Might he not have continued, and even have become more perfect?' I paused, uncertain how to say what was in my mind. 'He is wonderful,' I said at length, 'but he is also full of faults.'

If the doctor interpreted my comment as a test, he gave no sign of it. Without so much as a flutter in his eyelids – perhaps because he had considered the question many times previously – he answered: 'He is full of faults, and these are the defects of youth, which a more extended life might have resolved. And yet these weaknesses are a part of the effect, are they not? If you remove them from his work, you take away something which is essential to it, not something which prevents it from becoming fully itself.'

I confess that this was an argument to which I had not given much thought, but which I instantly saw was valuable. I nodded my head, as much to urge the doctor to continue as to show that I agreed with him.

'What I mean here is this. When we say the name "Keats", certain qualities and effects come into our mind, do they not? A certain density of description, a loadedness, voluptuary . . .'

'Mass,' I interrupted, taking up the litany. 'Softness,

dampness, luxury – yet also urgency and fire. A nobility of purpose and aim. Precisely. These are the things.'

'And are they not inseparable from youth? Suppose Keats had been spared, and continued working. It is clear from such writings as we have that latterly he grew impatient with himself, and sought a new direction. You have read that fragment of his "Hyperion", which his publisher falsely proclaimed was given up under the pressure of criticism. Does that not breathe a new spirit?'

I agreed that this was possible, and pointed out how the poem engaged with Milton, as Keats had not previously done, which affected the melody of the lines, as well as their thought. I believe I used some fanciful image, comparing the previous poems to the music of a harp, and 'Hyperion' to the more severe and grander notes of an organ – but the doctor forgave me this flight, and pressed forward.

'We cannot decide how this voice – this second Keats – would compare with the one we have. It may have been greater still; it may have been much less. The notion of having *an idea* in poetry had always been an enemy to him, unless it were made palpable, as a feeling, and "Hyperion" is founded on ideas which it is determined to express. Perhaps Keats would have forged a style to contain them, as I say; perhaps he would have been incapable.'

'Which leaves us . . .' I interrupted again, only to have the doctor cut across me with his own eagerness.

'Which leaves us bound to be grateful for what we have. And what we have is Keats – full of weaknesses, but also full of wonders. Anything else would have deserved another name.'

The doctor had reached a conclusion, and closed his eyes once more. I allowed myself to gaze on him as freely as I suppose he intended: the open shirt showing the lean neck; the mouth still nervous though in repose; the broad pale brow and scalp with its tonsure of gingerish hair. I had often remarked in my own patients how as they sickened and approached death, they assumed a look they had worn as children. So it was with the doctor. For all his talk of age, and its mixed blessing of disappointment and release, he appeared to me more and more clearly in the lineaments of youth. But it was youth expressing enervation and not optimism. Youth which knows its course of life is run.

While I still sat in silence, brooding upon this connection, a light pattering began on the window. My concentration on the doctor had been so intense, I had not noticed the weather change during our talk. Now as I looked about me, the room seemed dark enough to persuade me that twilight had come – which in truth was only rain, sweeping across the grazing in a heavy veil. The leaves on the myrtle were already bowed and shining, and the sheep – which had formerly been spread at an equal distance from one another – were bunched into a tight flock. I watched single drops of moisture coagulate on the glass until they formed distinct streams and rivulets, the process being a kind of enchantment.

When I looked back into the room Mrs Reilly had reappeared, bearing a lacquer tray on which stood a smoking pot of tea and cups. I rose at once, and helped her to place it on the table beside the doctor, whose eyes remained shut until our little ceremony of clanking and pouring was done. She and I did not exchange glances except once, when we smiled, like friends who know a secret that does not need to be spoken.

'Doctor?' Mrs Reilly had filled his cup so that it was but half tea and the remainder milk, and he rallied with the look of surprise I might have expected to see in someone who believed they had slept for several hours.

'Ah,' he said, pressing himself upright and (I supposed) regretting to be caught at a disadvantage. The harsh blush of discomfort, which I had noticed a moment before, was now mercifully faded from his cheeks. 'Forgive me, Dr Tabor. I am easily tired, and our visits . . .'

'I should leave you, Sir,' I said, fiddling with the middle button of my jacket and making as if to go. But my courtesy was dismissed, as I had hoped it would be.

'No, no,' he said. 'It is a reward of my condition that a catnap has the effect of several hours' sleep. We must continue.' I was understandably heartened by this, except that there followed an incident which, though small in itself, struck me with the force of tragedy. As the doctor went to take his cup from Mrs Reilly, he fumbled at the handle, knocking the contents half over himself and half upon the floor. Cooled though it was by the milk, the tea nevertheless burned him as it soaked through his shirt and onto the skin of his stomach and chest. I felt the pain as if it was on my own body, and jumped up while the doctor twisted on his chaise. 'Oh, Oh,' he cried, in the most

113

pitiable voice, and 'Oh, Oh' Mrs Reilly joined in, while we dabbed at him with our handkerchiefs, then undid his shirt to remove it.

The material was a soft white cotton, which had formerly covered him in folds, and as we peeled it away I noticed how effectively it had disguised his true shape. The chest was hideously emaciated, each rib starkly drawn, and the centre sunk into a deep declivity. A fresh wave of pity ran through me at this evidence of his frailty, now blotched with the irregular red shape of the spilled tea, and while Mrs Reilly hurried out to fetch him clean clothing, I drew the blanket up to his shoulders to cover him. 'I am sorry. I am sorry,' he said repeatedly, even more like a child than before, to which I could only reply that the sorrow was all mine, which indeed it was. In our conversations, I had been lulled by the abstract fascination of our subject into forgetting the doctor's humanity. It was now returned to me with a force that was close to embarrassment.

Mrs Reilly soon returned, re-clothed the doctor, held a fresh cup to his lips (from which he drank in large gulps, to prove that he was in command of himself), and eventually we settled down once again. Yet while everything seemed restored to its old place, in truth nothing was the same. A small but definite step had been taken; a frosty air of finality hung over our proceedings.

'Where were we?' asked the doctor, in the efficient voice of a man who knows he must conclude certain items of business. In the aftermath of such a distressing scene as the one I had just witnessed, I did not like to assume such a brisk manner myself, even though to shirk it would be a mark of disrespect. I therefore (after glancing at Mrs Reilly, who had by now taken her place at my side) braced myself to pursue my former candid indirection.

'We were speaking of Keats,' I said, 'and discussing the possible conditions of his afterlife.'

'Ah yes. His poems.'

'Not so much those,' I persevered, 'as how he would have lived.'

The doctor was evidently still shaken by his accident, and pressed one hand gently against his side, where the hot tea had burned him. 'Do you have an answer to that yourself?' he asked, playing for more time in which to consider his answer. His eyes swam away from my face to the window, where threads of moisture were still forming and dissolving on the glass. 'Rain! Rain! Rain!' he added wearily, his efficient manner suddenly deserting him. 'It would be a fit subject for a song, if someone would write it.'

'I do have an answer,' I replied quickly, before the direction of our talk was lost. 'My answer is that he would have felt the inevitable wasting of his gifts, and turned to other interests. He would have resumed his career as a physician, perhaps.'

'You say inevitable?'

'But I thought we had agreed. In our conversation about Wordsworth.'

'So we did,' said the doctor, still distracted. 'Very well, let us call it inevitable then, and let it pass. But to continue: do you not think it would be a fine thing to catch the countenance of a place in a piece of writing? This rain, for example, and this green field beyond. It is nothing yet it has a personality, if I may say so, an *intellect*. This is what we look for in Wordsworth, is it not. Why should we suppose such a vein of writing had been exhausted?'

'It has not been, I am sure,' I said, meaning to humour him in his perambulations, but also to keep my object in sight. I added: 'You are telling me that you think it impossible that Keats would have ceased writing?'

His eyes turned dreamily back to me. I had the impression of his illness sweeping through him in gusts, each soundless, but each lifting him a little nearer the end of his existence. Energy and lassitude, light and darkness, were competing within him, the lassitude and darkness gradually gaining control.

He gathered himself at last and spoke steadily, keeping the feeling in his voice to a minimum, but at the same time showing me, by the quiet clasping and unclasping of one hand upon the blanket, that he was speaking from the heart. 'I think,' he said, 'it is impossible that any man, however young, could set his mind on a certain ambition, and feel the power of a certain gift working within him, and later deny it entirely. Since such power might be considered a natural thing, such a refusal would be to deny nature. It cannot be done. It should not be done. And yet every mental pursuit takes its reality and worth from the ardour of the pursuer – so if the pursuer should falter, why . . .'

'The reality alters,' I offered. 'The worth changes.'

'That is my contention. We have said before that

116

human life may be compared to a large mansion of many apartments – it is a favourite conceit of mine. Keats had not the time, nor the opportunity, to explore beyond the second or third chamber of this mansion – where, if he had been blessed by circumstance, he would have enjoyed release from the perplexities of weighing good with evil.'

'How a release?'

'He would have perhaps felt the balance of the two could be resolved. I do not mean by ignorance. I mean by devoting himself to a definite cause.'

'In the world?'

'In the world, as you say.' The doctor steadied himself, then resumed with determination. 'His whole life, such as it may be counted a life, was a kind of Prologue, dedicated to study and preparation for an unseen end. While his genius remained, that end was poetry, and progress towards it seemed quite natural. When the genius faded – because it must, or because the unique circumstances upon which it depended were altered – might not a different but compatible end have come in view? I say it again: he was a man much preoccupied by the spirit of exploration, one to whom application and study and thought were as meat and drink – yet whose dedication to poetry still allowed him to think there was something wanting in a man who passes his life among books and thoughts on books. Might he not, upon entering apartments which in his youth had been far off, have chosen to dedicate himself to the happiness of others and not the expression of his self? Might not his silent studies – supposing he had a healthy and lasting organisation of heart

117

and lungs – have demanded this?'

Although the doctor had ended with a question, I did not feel constrained to give him a reply, nor did he seem to expect one. He lay with eyes closed, hands now draped limply across his chest, breathing in such extremely shallow sips that I supposed he might even have fallen asleep. With a part of myself, I was concerned that I had contributed to his exhaustion. Yet Mrs Reilly's continuing silence, and the fact that she had not stirred from her seat, informed me that the doctor had only done as he himself wished. He had once again spoken not so much in the manner of a conversation as of a man giving an address – a murmured address, an address closing in a whisper, but a considered thing for all that. This allowed me to believe it was not merely frailty that I saw in his posture, but something akin to fulfilment. He had wished to unburden himself, and was satisfied by his performance.

With this in mind, I considered how best to present my next and final parcel of questions. As I did so, casting my eyes round the room so as to imprint its various details on my memory to such a depth that I would never forget them, I heard the rain slacken against the window, and saw a single broad beam of sunlight strike into the grazing. Immediately, as if triggered by a mechanism, a thrush began singing. For a moment I supposed it was the linnet in its cage, but when I turned to look I found this creature still in its habitual dowdy huddle. The notes of the thrush's song continued to strengthen, until they seemed a downpour to match the one which had just ceased.

'A thrush.' It was the doctor, speaking as if he had read

my mind, but with a catch of laughter. 'He has come to prove me wrong. He is announcing to the winds that nothing natural can be denied.'

'That is not a contradiction,' I said, also smiling. 'If what you say about the various apartments is true, it would have been an entirely natural thing to convert the health-giving powers of poetry into a more practical care for the happiness of others.' I regretted my words, which seemed ponderous following his own, but consoled myself that it had become my task, even my duty, to wring the last drops of interest from our talk. It was a guilty thought, and all the more so when the doctor answered with a perceptibly greater degree of weariness in his voice. I saw that whatever satisfactions my questions might provide him with, I could not expect to continue much longer. There was a weakness – a presence filling the entire room – which made every moment more painful. Yet the doctor seemed so much at ease, and so accepting of his condition, that it was still not alarm I felt but a busy determination.

At the same time, I still had a responsibility to his condition, and shifted in my chair. 'I shall soon be gone,' I said.

'No,' the doctor replied with a morbid smile. 'I shall soon be gone. You will remain, and remember what I have said.' It was spoken with such speed, and in such a throw-away manner, that I did not immediately feel its weight. When I did so, I veered even more wildly in my mind between the knowledge that I should leave him, and the conviction that I should persevere.

After her long silence, it was Mrs Reilly who now spoke to reassure me. 'A little longer will do no harm,' she said in her soft burr, then affectionately touched her finger-ends on the edge of the doctor's chaise. I looked sideways at her but she ignored me, fixing her whole attention on the doctor.

'Very well,' I said, with the odd sensation of being at once intimate with their world and quite outside it, which aggravated the awkwardness of my speech. 'Let us suppose that his poetry disappeared. Do you mean the writing of it or the publishing of it?' I had not liked to mention the name Keats again so soon, as will have been noticed.

The doctor said nothing, and after a while of supposing that he was preparing a reply, I discovered that he did not mean to give one. It was, I realised, the first instance of his refusing my interrogation. I changed my direction, and spoke again.

'And what of plays, then. Keats had an interest in plays, did he not?'

'Oh, plays,' he said, with a disparaging half-groan. 'Many a poet has squandered his talents in the theatre. Plays are not the thing.'

'You might not say so if they were successful, and made money.'

'That is true. We could, if we were so minded, name a number of poets who have been lifted out of a mess by a tragedy. And yet for the case we are discussing . . .' He faltered briefly, then continued. 'Keats had a passion for plays, you are right, and for Shakespeare in particular, which did indeed lead him to experiment with the form. Let us say, charitably, that he recognised the existence of something dramatic in his own character. That part of him was not the dominant part, no matter what his ambitions told him; it was merely excited by the requirements of the moment.'

'The need to live, you mean?' I asked, keeping the bright tone I had adopted.

'The need for the means to live, yes. He was too inward a man for the theatre.'

'What of letters, then?'

'What of them?' the doctor asked, with a sudden bridling severity.

'Letters may be published,' I answered plainly.

He returned my words to me in the same tone. 'Letters may indeed be published, and we may enjoy reading them. But they will never please us unless they were truly written in private, with no thoughts of a large audience. In this way they are not the same as poetry, which surprises by looking inwards and outwards at once. Poetry is a kind of Janus.'

I understood from this that the doctor meant to return to speaking of abstract literary matters, which was not my intention. I therefore risked an insulting frankness.

'Very well, Sir,' I said. 'Let me ask you a simple question. You give me to believe that Keats might have come back to England, that the good genius of his poetry might have left him, and that he devoted himself instead to the welfare of others. Why could he not have done this as himself? Why go to ground, in the disguise of a different name, in the refuge of a strange place?'

'If you ask that,' the doctor flicked back at me, 'you have understood nothing.'

I was shocked by this anger, and confused for a moment. 'No; I have understood . . .'

The doctor interrupted me, 'Because he was too much identified with one thing. With his poetry.'

'But . . .' I began, still gathering my wits. 'That is to say art exists in a world of its own, and has no connection with anything around it. We have already said that is not true. We have decided art is salubrious.'

The doctor hunched his shoulders a little, as if squaring up for physical combat, yet his voice now softened into a tone that suggested pity rather than rage. 'I have not made myself clear. I meant to say: the man who pins the whole notion of himself on one achievement might have to become a different man, if that achievement were to fail.' A bleak smile flashed across his face. 'Your question seems to imply there should have been some great event in his life, to make him change his name as well as his direction. A woman perhaps, or some disgrace or other trouble. My contention is: it could have been some less obvious but equally decisive thing. He might have changed his name because he had despaired of his original self.'

I nodded slowly at this, feeling the great weight of sadness which lay behind the doctor's words, and knowing that in a different mood – a *usual* mood, I should like to think – they would have brought me to a halt, out of sympathy. But in the present, exceptional and (as I kept reminding myself) terminal situation, I pressed on. 'Very well,' I said. 'Let me put to you another set of practical questions. Supposing Keats had lived, as he has begun to do in our imaginations, what of his friends? A man may change in himself but he cannot abolish his whole society.'

As I spoke, Mrs Reilly drew her feet more closely together and tucked a stray wisp of her red hair beneath her cap. By this modest gesture she confirmed what I already knew: that my question was the boldest I had yet asked, and therefore also the one most likely to distress the doctor. I was prepared for her to intervene at any moment.

'It is true,' the doctor said, speaking with deliberate slowness, laying down his words like the planks of a bridge, onto which he ventured over an abyss. 'And yet if a man's need is sufficient he may alter it substantially, retaining a few representatives of his former life to protect the mystery of his new one. If those few are as good as their word, and discreet, a reinvention would be possible.' There was another pause, and the doctor ran the tip of his tongue, which was yellowish, around his lips. When he resumed, it was with more alacrity. 'Think of Coleridge,' he said. 'Did he not resign his familiar existence when as a young man he joined the Dragoons, which I believe was the case?'

'But Coleridge did not conceal his whole life,' I protested, with the same unbecoming frankness. Such was the quality of the silence now emanating from Mrs Reilly, I chose to affect a more blustering manner, which was intended to prove I had no serious intent. Nevertheless, I felt the air of the room pressing around us tightly, and knew that it must soon break.

'It is the same principle,' said the doctor, seeing his escape was blocked, and speaking again in a hushed voice.

'Very well,' I replied, maintaining the same relaxed tone. 'Let us keep the case of Keats as our example. Joseph Severn, who nursed him in Rome, would certainly have been a party to the secret, and no doubt others in the English Colony as well. Indeed, they would have agreed to more than keeping a secret. They would have had to prac- tise a deception.'

The doctor sighed, but the expansion of his chest did not affect the arrangement of his shirt, so slight was it.

'It is not easy to imagine such a pretence being main- tained,' I went on regardless. 'Talkers will always talk. You may throw the smallest pebble into a lake, but its ripples will reach the furthest shore.'

The doctor came back to me in the same diminished voice. 'Joseph Severn is still living,' he said. 'Whatever Joseph Severn knew he still knows. And he was but one among many exceptional friends. Others may have loved as deeply, but none proved it better.'

I was grateful for the doctor's reply, notwithstanding its seeming like an answer which was no answer. I took from it such suggestions as existed, and continued.

'And what of others he had known in England? Reynolds? Woodhouse? Brown? What of his publishers, too? What of Hunt?'

The doctor pressed his head backwards into the chaise, as if really frightened by my question, and recoiling from it. As his eyes widened, the irises seemed unnaturally small and hard in the large O of their whites. 'You must recollect,' he said quickly, 'Keats was not always at ease, even in the company of friends. He would often protest that his general life in society was silence – that in society he had lived under an everlasting restraint except when composing. If you are concerned about his friends, as I see you are, I urge you to entertain the notion that he was capable of tiring of men and things, and of considering that days alone, if they were filled with speculations, were bearable or even pleasant. Does that comfort you?'

The doctor's wide eyes were now turned on me with such a beseeching look, I could not but feel remorse, and anger with myself. 'Of course,' I told him. 'Of course it does.' But my answer did not pacify him entirely. As a final shot in his defence, he fired off:

'Any man may hate the world, and wish himself rid of it, as it batters the wings of his self-will.'

He was now breathing rapidly, and I saw I had over-stepped an invisible mark. Mrs Reilly abruptly stood up, smoothing her dress with an impatient sweep of her hand, and bustled to the head of the doctor's chaise, where she stood behind him, allowing herself a full view of me. She drew a handkerchief from her cuff (it had a pretty border, decorated with red silk) and wiped it across the whole of the doctor's face. He blinked his eyes heavily and thanked her, making a sign for her to seat herself again. She did not, but regarded me steadily. There was no enmity in her gaze, but a kind of fierce tenderness, as though begging me to take pity. This was not, I deduced, to deter me from my course entirely, but to demand more tact than before.

After a considerable silence, in which the doctor swallowed once or twice, making a gluey sound in his throat, he asked a question of his own. His voice quavered, though whether through weakness or emotion I could not immediately decide.

'And what of his family?' he said, and swallowed once more. When he continued, his voice gradually strengthened, evidently driven onwards by a desperate kind of anger and mortification. 'His brother and his sister. In such a case as we are devising, the sacrifice would be immense. To imagine the grief of loved ones, who really believed him dead, and to know that he could have ended their suffering with a word. To follow the course of their lives and yet always be hidden from them, and never to share their disappointments or their pleasures. To live entirely on the outside of oneself . . .' He hesitated again, his eyes reddening. 'It would require a barbarous kind of spirit, would it not. It would require cruelty.'

I hesitated, astonished by this sudden eruption, which contained the very questions I wished to ask myself. Indeed, our roles were now briefly altered: he was the inquisitor and I, in a flurry of something like panic, the anxious audience. Not so anxious, however, that I abandoned my purpose altogether.

'But if . . .' I stopped and glanced at Mrs Reilly, who was now biting her lip in an evident torment of indecision, not knowing whether to let the doctor continue, or restrain and so protect him. 'But if . . .' I said again.

'But if,' the doctor broke in, 'but if the sacrifice was deemed valuable, you are going to say?' He rolled his head miserably to and fro. 'That would be the sole justification. If the new life, the afterlife as we may call it, could be considered important, then the sacrifice . . .'

The doctor's argument had closed to such a tight circle of reasoning that he could not continue without repeating himself. I hesitated again, although I feared that only minutes of his company remained, and was exceedingly reluctant to lose any chance of illumination.

'Forgive me,' I said, concealing my intentions behind a cloak of stupidity. 'But if we are to take these conjectures as fact, I must repeat a question I have already asked. Namely: why should not Keats have returned to England as himself, either as soon as he regained his health, or eventually. Could not some parts of the sacrifice have then been avoided?'

The doctor's eyes were dull as stones. 'It is not a simple objection,' he said. 'If a new life, and a new name, were indeed his choice, we must ask ourselves what deep wounds, and what pride, underlay it.'

'Pride?' I echoed, in real puzzlement.

'Pride,' he repeated. 'The pride which had been gored when he knew that his great ambition had been frustrated – that he had failed to become the person he wished.'

'It is not pride you are describing now but humiliation.'

'Call it what you will.' The doctor's voice had now dropped still further, so that he seemed to be speaking from the deepest part of his throat, and to be incapable of projecting any mood save for flat melancholy. He blinked at me, which allowed me to notice that his eyes were moist with unfallen tears. 'I mean,' he went on bravely, 'that turbulence of self which occurs when our best aims are thwarted. To give a chapter and verse to this only increases the sense of how unnecessary such turbulence might be. To speak of it as spoiled hopes, the unkindness of critics, the exhaustions of poverty, the tribulations of love: these things are diminished by time. But in the heat of their first appearance, they seem the very definition of existence. Any number of decisions might be reached, which seem just when they are acted upon, but which time might prove foolish.'

'Very well,' I said, with a sincere reluctance to add to the unhappiness now coursing through him, but still with an equal reluctance to draw our conversation to a close. 'This feeling – this pride, or this humiliation: let us suppose it formed his decision to change. What then? Were there not still a thousand later chances to revise it? Not to have done so would have been to live an afterlife of continuous regret. It would be unbearable.'

'Unbearable sadness,' said the doctor, at last looking away from me, and slowly clenching his hands. When he had made this gesture before, it had been to hold them shut for only a moment before relaxing them again. Now he kept them balled tightly into fists, like a boxer. The veins crawling between his knuckles stood out distinct and sluggish. 'That is why I prefer to speak of pride,' he said. 'In such a situation as this, where a man might feel that his original motives were sensible and good, but lives to see time prove them a mistake, pride may become a sort of comfort. I am not speaking of vanity, now, which may have been present at first, but of the superior kind of pride. Of self-belief. The comfort of knowing, as each day ends, that whatever the cost to the do-er, the work done is useful.'

When the doctor finished, Mrs Reilly leaned slowly forward and rested her fingertips on the doctor's shoulders, as if she might transmit her own energy into his body. I would have done the same, had I not become so engrossed. To speak plainly: my wish to force the doctor to a confession overwhelmed all my other considerations. In my defence, I can only add that I felt the doctor himself had given me reasons to believe our conversation might serve a greater good.

Accordingly, I nerved myself to ask one further question – one that I had previously not dared to put, and had even hesitated to frame, it seemed so likely to give offence. Precisely as my mouth opened to begin, the doctor himself seized the very thought that was in my mind, speaking with a stone-steadiness which indicated the extreme strength of his feeling.

'And supposing,' he said, 'there were one person in particular on whom he had come to feel his happiness might depend? How do we imagine that loss, Dr Tabor? How do we do that?' His agitation was now so visible, like a current running beneath his skin, that I did not believe he would continue. His hands had tightened to a marble whiteness, and his eyes stared with the terror a man might show on viewing a terrible monstrosity or crime. But with an effort of self-control, or of self-punishment, that seemed remarkable at the time and now seems wholly astonishing, he added: 'What do we say as we imagine him watching her grieve, then recover, then perhaps marry another and be happy, and travel through the world? Do we suppose the reasons for his hiding, however noble in themselves, could endure such a torment? Do we believe that public good is worth such a private hell?'

The doctor rolled his head as he finished speaking, and his fingers uncurled, seizing the blanket so that I believed he might fling it aside and attempt to rise. But to do what? To strike me, I thought, not so much for what I had said, as to release the storm inside him. Mrs Reilly slid her palms down flat on his shoulders, gripping him and making a low crooning noise which was more like weeping than comfort.

I was so shocked by this spectacle I immediately regretted my part in its production, as I do to this day. 'I know of no such woman,' I said, in a voice of blank fearfulness. 'But you are right. Supposing one existed, we cannot imagine it. It is too dreadful.'

'Too dreadful. Too dreadful,' the doctor echoed, his own voice rising to a high sing-song wail, and his head tossing to and fro again so that he seemed oblivious of who he was, and of Mrs Reilly and myself. 'Too dreadful. Too dreadful,' he repeated. The agony in his voice was like a blade; I shall never forget it.

'Mrs Reilly,' I said loudly, rising to my feet in a fluster. 'We have finished. I have been remiss.'

She darted me a look, not angry, but aghast at the sorrow she had heard in the doctor's voice. Then she fixed all her attention on him. I did so too, and in my mind's eye I do so again now, remembering that this was the last time I saw him plainly. The effort of his last few remarks had brought to the surface everything in him that was raw and vulnerable, so that his very skin seemed to shine with a transparent thinness, like a coating of wax. Had it not been for the breath whistling between his lips, and the flickering of his eyelids as they at last began to narrow over his eyes, I might even have thought that death had already come to him. But there was no arguing with that stricken and persistent breathing: it was still strong enough to shake a white thread of saliva, stretched across the corner of his mouth.

I do not mean to suggest, in mentioning these details, that I found anything about the doctor's appearance in the least repellent. On the contrary. As I regarded his wasted features I took them into my heart for ever.

I do not know how long I continued in this reverie – probably no more than a few seconds. When I came back to myself, Mrs Reilly was already speaking. 'You have done too much,' she was saying, still without any anger, but with an unflinching steadiness. 'You are right. We have done too much. Too much.' I did not have the opportunity at that moment to thank her for making her small alteration to my phrase – only to enjoy a flash of gratitude, and to tell myself again that the doctor had only said what he wished to say.

Or so I have since tried to persuade myself a thousand

times, without ever once entirely believing it to be the case. It has become the burden of uncertainty I must carry, which oppresses each day and every action. In my pursuit of the doctor's story – I should more properly say of his *opinion* – I betrayed my responsibilities as a physician.

As one result, among many, my final minutes in the doctor's house were not as I had expected them to be. I had entertained thoughts of a gentle and courteous leave-taking, with promises – however implausible – of further visits and pleasant hours. In fact my departure was sudden. Still speaking in the same dispassionate voice (though muffled as she stooped over the doctor, pressing her handkerchief to his mouth), Mrs Reilly informed me that I could be of most use by fetching Dr Garrett, as I had done before. I told her I would do so at once, yet stood by for a moment, without moving, hoping that I might have one further clear view of the doctor, and the chance to make plain my admiration and affection for him. But this was not to be. As Mrs Reilly continued to bend over him, I could do no more than glimpse his face over her shoulder – desperately white and agape, like the face of a drowning man. The air was smothering him rather than giving life, and although his eyes lighted on my own, I do not believe that he saw me, still less recognised me as a friend.

'Quickly, Dr Tabor,' Mrs Reilly whispered to me, and I stepped to her side. 'We are waiting for you. Go.'

'Dr Cake,' I said, but the face gave no sign in return. Impulsively – for it seemed a more intimate gesture than

I had earned the right to give – I bent quickly forward so that my sleeve actually brushed against Mrs Reilly, and laid my open hand on his brow. A sensation returned to me that I had first experienced on shaking his hand at our original meeting, though now more powerful than ever; his skin was like hot ice, as if I had touched the warmth of his brain itself. That, too, is a thing I shall never forget. I believe that I may have uttered some further words, but they were not significant. Even before I had reached the door, Mrs Reilly had knelt down and taken him in her arms, lying lightly across him, and his own arms had crept around her shoulders, very slack and lifeless.

By the time I had made my way (as rapidly as possible) to Dr Garrett and seen him depart for the doctor's house, and then returned to my room at the inn, it was too late in the evening for me to contemplate leaving the village until the following morning. I therefore made the necessary arrangements, and settled in my room to review the experience of the past few hours. The busy noises of the street gave every appearance of calm: the scrape of the horses' shoes as they ascended or descended its slope, the occasional greetings of neighbours rising into the air like smoke. Yet such were the sights I had seen, and the feelings I had entertained, I could not compose my mind.

My agitation was all the greater for knowing I had not made an adequate farewell. Indeed, I feared that in my haste I had demolished the fragile structure upon which the whole of my communication with the doctor had depended. Try as I might to recapture the better part of our meeting, it therefore became the occupation of my evening to recollect its end. As if I were watching the antics of a stranger, I saw the doctor's prints and books pass before me in a swirling kaleidoscope when I went to open the door of his study for the final time. I heard the definite soft *tok* as it closed behind me. I felt the darkness of the hall slide off my face like cobwebs as I stepped outside into the surprising sunlight. I watched myself set off down the drive: the gravel and small stones rattling underfoot, the tree-shadows swimming over my eyes, and the metal catch of the gate.

There was no opportunity to turn and look back at the house – it was imperative that I made haste. Yet I did turn and look: the windows were blind with sky, the white façade a complete blank. I felt as I have often done in my professional capacity, examining the exterior of a man's head which to all appearances is healthy, but which knowledge tells me contains some contamination of disease or derangement. The house was a perfect mask – impervious and unperturbed as all Nature is, when tragedy affects some particular part of it. The trees continued to wave their leaves. The clouds rolled through the heavens. The little birds and other creatures persevered with their rustling lives in the undergrowth. They were not in the least concerned with me – with my thoughts, or with the errand I must immediately perform. I left the gate swinging on its hinges, and continued my half-walk, half-run to Dr Garrett.

FIVE

The last two items in the Tabor/Cake Archive are letters, both written by Cake's housekeeper Mrs Reilly in
a simple, rounded script. The first covers both sides of
a single sheet of white paper edged with black, which
is stamped at the head with Cake's address. It is dated
4 September 1844, ten days after Cake's funeral.

Dear Dr Tabor,

Thank you for your note of condolence, and for the suc-
cinct article you wrote for the *Messenger*. It has been much
appreciated, not least by myself, who understands better
than anyone the difficulties of your task. Now that it has
been performed, I hope that we may turn to other things.

You will have noticed, I think, that my own health is not
perfect, but I mean to remain as long as possible in this
house, which the doctor in his kindness has allowed me to
call my own. If ever your work brings you towards
Woodham, you would be welcome to call on me. The doctor felt a special pleasure in your visits, and so would I.

Yours truly
Aileen Reilly

The second letter is written on the same type of white paper, but appears faintly creased, as though it had long ago been crumpled and smoothed out. It is dated 22 October 1849, more than five years after Cake's death and less than a week before Mrs Reilly's own. (She died on 26 October 1849, and was buried close to Cake in the graveyard at St Mary's, Woodham.) It seems to have been written fast; the ink is almost see-through, and the letters shakily large:

Dear Wm.,

Please find herewith the packet of which we have often spoken during your visits, which I mean to give you when you call again this p.m. Now that we both understand my time is short, my mind is made up. It will be yours for you to do with it as you decide.

A.R.

AFTERWORD

I said in my Foreword that Cake would be left to speak for himself, or to be shown as Tabor found him. But certain questions – about his teasings and evasions, as well as his compulsive declarations – have to be faced. So to start with the most obvious: how many of the facts in his story coincide with the facts of John Keats's life?

A good many. Like Cake, Keats was born in 1795, went to school near London, was apprenticed to an apothecary, and began to study medicine at Guy's Hospital, where he worked as a dresser to the great surgeon Astley Cooper. He seemed set on a safe – even a distinguished – career. But then he interrupted his training. He devoted himself to writing and, as part of a determined effort to 'get experience', undertook a walking tour – which included a visit to Ireland – with his friend Charles Brown. By the time he returned to London he had already developed symptoms of tuberculosis, and for the next two years struggled against the disease as also he wrote the poems by which he is remembered. The poems which found so few contemporary admirers, and sold so badly. In the autumn of 1820, in a last desperate attempt to regain his health, he

137

sailed to Italy – and died there, in Rome, the following spring, aged twenty-five.

And then? Then the slow burn of his reputation. The ignition. The dazzling rocket-climb of his fame. All the world knows that, just as all the world knows the tragic story of his life. But not Tabor. His Keats sailed for Italy but recovered, and 'jumped down Etna for some public good'. His Keats returned to England and finished his training. His Keats gave up his old life, his old friends, and went to ground. His Keats never wrote, or at least never published, another line of poetry. His Keats sacrificed his writing for the sake of his patients. His Keats eventually sickened a second time, and was carried indoors from the garden by the only people who accepted his afterlife.

It's easy to see why Tabor wanted to believe that Cake was Keats. It's a marvellous notion in itself – a sensational surprise – but it has an extra attraction too. The pathos of Keats's early death is so intense, the idea that he might in fact have been spared seems to right a wrong. We feel that such a genius, and such a heroic human being, simply *ought* to have lived for longer. And Tabor clearly thought this was a practical possibility. As a doctor, he would certainly have come across patients in Finchley – even tubercular or cancerous patients – whose illnesses were suddenly and inexplicably cured. Why should Keats not have been like them?

But in truth it's difficult to be sure what Tabor did believe. He seems to have started his Woodham diary thinking he might publish it, and astonish the world with his discovery. Then somewhere along the line he changed his mind, and preferred to keep everything to himself.

Why? What was he up to? There are a number of possibilities. Perhaps he decided that the doctor was not Keats after all. Everything Cake revealed about himself – about his beliefs, his habits, his circumstances – were things Keats might have said, had he lived. They were plausible. But that still didn't mean they were true. The whole performance might have been a gigantic con-trick, or the wild projection of a dying man. Maybe, in spite of Cake's insinuations, and the scraps of expert knowledge he sprinkled through his talk, he was just playing a game, and Tabor realised this when he looked over the pages he had written.

On the other hand Tabor might have had reasons for believing Cake – not just reasons based on the evidence he saw and heard, but other reasons that we can only guess. Reasons to do with those parts of his life which have never been written and never can be written. Reasons like insecurity and fear. And ambition. In the past, his few readers have assumed his poetic aims were pretty modest. Now, thanks to the last two letters in the Archive, we can't be sure. What was the 'packet' that Mrs Reilly mentioned? It might have been nothing but a sentimental memento – a much-loved book, perhaps, or one of Cake's Classical prints. But no one who has read Tabor's description of the scene by the fire-side can help wondering whether Mrs Reilly saved some papers from the flames, which she then passed to Tabor. And if she did, what sort of papers were they? Documents, or poems? And if poems, were they by Cake or Keats? When the fuzz of questions reaches this point, it completely obscures the 'old' Tabor.

Which is not to say the new Tabor then stands clearly before us. Looked at from one point of view, he is changed from a good public servant who loved poetry into a thief and a forger. He is guilty of something breath-taking: of publishing, under his own name, the poems that Keats wrote in his secret middle age. From a different perspective, he becomes a complicated kind of hero. His affection for Cake was so evident, Cake trusted him with a secret that he had kept from all but his very closest friends and family. We must admire Tabor for this, and therefore be prepared to think differently about his motives in publishing *Hyperion and Other Poems*. Cake – and then Mrs Reilly – put him in an impossible position by all-but asking him to publish 'late' poems by Keats which he knew weren't up to the standard of the early and 'real' poems. And he solved the dilemma by taking the burden of failure on himself. That's to say: the decision to publish the poems under his own name wasn't so much an act of appropriation as a form of protection.

Whichever way we look at it, Tabor can't help seeming a little foolish. He could never have got away with his deception for ever. Someone would find him out and tell on him: they always do. But he has got away with it, until now. Everyone who has been through his papers before me – the medical men, and the few literary types like his editor Greene – has either not noticed the connections with Keats, or chosen to keep quiet about them.

Once again: if they did choose to keep quiet, why?

Presumably because they thought the idea was preposterous or un-provable. They would have been right on both counts – but that isn't the point. The important thing is not just whether Cake and Keats were the same person, but how much difference it would make if they had been.

To put it another way: supposing *Hyperion and Other Poems* really was by Keats, how much damage had Tabor done? When the book came out in early 1850, a few weeks before Tabor died, reviewers all damned it with faint praise. Most of them mentioned Keats, which was hardly surprising in view of the title and the language. But where, thirty-odd years earlier, they had savaged 'excess', now they thought it was less than it might have been. Less thrilling. Less 'luxurious in its pantings and slitherings', as the *Quarterly Review* said. If Tabor read those verdicts, he probably felt disappointed. But at the same time he would have enjoyed seeing 'little Keats' – young Keats – getting his just deserts at last. Furthermore, if he had been motivated by generosity, rather than something more venal, he would have felt that his decision had been validated.

Perhaps he understood something else as well. If Cake really had been Keats, and had thrown off his mask at some point and published under his own name, the result would not finally have been any different. Of course it would have been in the short term. There would have been gasps of astonishment in the newspapers. Detective-style sleuthings. Journalists dispatched to Italy to interview Joseph Severn, to St Louis to track down his brother George, across Europe on the trail of Fanny Brawne (who had married and become Fanny Lindo in 1833). But when the fuss died down, everything would have been the same, or nearly the same. Cool heads would have re-drawn the map of literary history – not that they would have needed to do much. They would have said about 'late Keats' what they said about late Tabor. That it was sub-Keats, not true Keats.

In other words, Tabor achieved two things – opposite things. He preserved the familiar shape of Keats's story by never publishing any account of his meetings with Cake, and by acting as a decoy for criticism. At the same time, he took the trouble to preserve the transcript of their con-versations – hoping, maybe, that one day they would see the light of day. It was an elegant solution to his predica-ment. It allowed him to be both a silent witness and the bearer of strange news – which it still does today. As far as Keats is concerned, Tabor preserves the ambiguous gift of tragedy. As far as we his readers are concerned, he nour-ishes the most beautiful of all deceptions. The illusion that we too might be able to cheat our own death.